Stalked A Collection of Thrillers

Louise Krieg

Published by Trellis Publishing, 2021.

STALKED

LOUISE KRIEG

The flash of Tasha's camera covered the rapidly stiffening body on the ground in front of her in a momentary pure white sheen. She studied the image on the LCD screen before bringing the viewfinder up to her eye again. Another burst of pure white blanketed the deceased.

She nearly dropped her camera when a voice startled her from behind.

"I got me one of those a while back," it said in an authoritative tone she'd come to associate with cops.

Tasha didn't need to turn around to know it was Vince standing behind her. He liked to creep up on her, and she was getting real sick of it.

"Oh?" she replied uninterested, kneeling down to get a different angle of the body. It was uncommonly hot for so early in the day, and she could feel the first bead of sweat trickle down her back. The protective coverall she was wearing spun tight over her legs as she kneeled, creating a human shaped oven for her to bake in.

Vince went on talking for some time about the DSLR he found at a great price online, bursting with pride at how he practically swindled the seller, some kid from Washington who needed the cash. Tasha didn't say anything. She was immersed in her routine of brief flashes, checks, angle adjustments, focusing the lens, another flash—

"Tasha?" Vince asked, still behind her, a hint of annoyance in his voice.

"Huh?" she turned around.

"I asked if you'd like to get some dinner tonight."

She stared at him mutely for a few seconds. His resilience was commendable. She'd turned him down probably a hundred times before, yet here he was again, a look of absolute self-importance on his face as he expected her to do nothing but agree to his offer. But she wasn't about to be swindled out of her time and self-respect as easily as that kid with the camera.

"Sorry, Vince," she said, knowing full well she sounded anything but sorry, "I told you, I don't go out with cops."

The self-importance turned an ashy grey on his face.

"One of these days I won't take no for an answer anymore," he said. The corners of his mouth twitched into what she could only describe as a snarl.

"Eh- excuse me?" she asked, incredulous.

Vince took a step closer to her, the stench of cigarettes and cheap cologne wafting off him like the heat on the pavement. She'd never been this close to him before, and she noticed a small piece of something green caught in his teeth.

"You prance around with your little camera," he said, cigarettes and garlic on his breath, "All serious and uninterested in anything else. Life's gonna run right by you, honey."

Tasha forced herself not to take a step back. She straightened her spine and looked him dead in the eyes.

"Don't call me *honey*," she said, struggling to keep her voice under control.

A serpentine smile spread on Vince's face. It would have been more effective had the piece of green garnish not been stuck in his yellowing teeth.

"I'm just saying," he shrugged, "You of all people should know that there are bad characters creeping around out there. The work we do shows us the ass-end of the world and the people crawling over it. We need each other."

He ran his cigarette stained fingers over the back of Tasha's hand. The sensation made her skin crawl, and for the second time that day she nearly dropped her camera. She snapped her hand back, fighting the ever growing urge to step away from him. If she retreated now he would see it as some sign of weakness.

"Vince," she said softly, keeping her voice low despite the fact that none of the other cops and crime scene investigators around them could hear their conversation, "I told you, I don't date cops, so stop asking."

The undercurrent of threat which loomed just beneath the look of semi-playfulness on his face came to the foreground quicker than the pure white light she draped over murder victims.

"I won't stop asking, *honey*," he said, emphasising the word with malicious intent.

Her own anger seethed inside.

"Not if you're the last guy on earth," she spat.

Tasha finally gave in to the urge to get away from him. She turned around and stomped off on shaky legs, biting her lower lip to fight off the tears threatening to well in her eyes. She didn't look back at him as she stowed her equipment in the white CSI van. But if she had, the look of resentment and determination on his face as he stood watching her would have made her blood run cold even in the baking heat.

...

"...hospitals are currently overcrowded. The Centre for Disease Control has asked that anyone showing flu-like symptoms please report to their nearest town hall for examination. Multiple cases of—"

Tasha flicked off the news, surprised at how utterly dark it was inside her bedroom without the artificial glare of the television. She lay in the dark for a while, staring into nothing, her brain firing at what felt like double speed. People were dying. *A lot* of people were dying. Her familiarity with dead bodies did nothing to make the thought of the rows upon rows of corpses lying under those stark white sheets in the glaring sun any more bearable. It was just a glimpse, a fleeting image caught on camera by one of the news anchors flying over the St. Bernadine hospital downtown. A big open stretch of lawn most probably previously used by doctors and patients for a reprise from the sterilised chemically bleached halls of the hospital was now being used as a storage space for victims of a virus which at first seemed like nothing but the common cold. How many bodies were there? A hundred? Two hundred? How many more in the hospital morgue?

Her cell phone vibrated next to her head. UNKNOWN NUMBER the caller ID read.

"Hello?" her phone was cool against her cheek.

There was no reciprocal greeting from the other side, just the faint electric hum of the connection.

"Hello?" she said again, a bit louder this time.

The phone beeped in her ear as the caller hung up.

She looked at the screen quizzically for a few seconds before putting the thing on silent. She lay in the dark for a while longer, thinking about the dead, before falling into a deep fitful sleep.

Her dreams were filled with white sheets. They covered everything, cars, benches, mailboxes, even the buildings. Every now and then the wind would pick up and lift one of the corners, revealing a decaying and rotting structure beneath. In the dream, Tasha shielded her eyes from the glare of the sheets baking in the sun. The light was extremely bright, but she felt no heat whatsoever. The light started to flicker, suddenly growing brighter in an instant and then fading away again. From somewhere far away she could hear a high pitched noise, then the flash of light again.

Tasha's eyes sprang open, only to have a bright flash of light nearly blind her. The flash was followed by the high pitched tone of a camera flash charging. Another flash of light and she was seeing stars floating on her bedroom ceiling.

"What—" she was confused and still thick with sleep. Was she still dreaming? No, another stab of light in her eyes and the unmistakable sound of the camera flash recharging was too real. And so was the weight on top of her. Someone was straddling her, trapping her in the light blanket she'd crawled under before going to sleep.

She wanted to scream, but it was as if her voice never existed. She momentarily completely forgot how to make even the simplest of sounds. She tried to heave the figure off her, but the blanket was spun tight around her legs and she could barely get them an inch off the mattress. The camera kept flashing in her face, and she had the sudden insane thought that somehow she was dead, and it was a CSI taking photographs of her corpse, gathering evidence of whatever brutal end she'd suffered. That thought alone was enough to give her a kind of strength she didn't know she had. Tasha dug her fingers into the mattress and gave a mighty shove upwards with her hips, knocking her assailant to the side, giving her just enough leeway to tuck her feet in, lift her knees, and throw him off completely.

There was a thud and a scramble as he hit the floor. She finally found her voice and screamed as loud as she could. She fumbled for the bedside lamp, her hands shaking and her fingers useless. In her panic she knocked it onto the floor, dying a little inside at the sound of the bulb shattering on the tiles. She vaulted out of bed to the other side, finding the light switch for the ensuite bathroom, and flicked it on. A few feet of dim yellow light streamed into the room. It was enough for her to see the intruder's silhouette as he fled through the doorway, camera in hand. She heard his heavy footsteps race down the hallway before her front door slammed shut.

It was only later, after she'd barred the door and phoned the police with no answer, that she stopped trembling. All the lights in her house were turned on. She sat cross legged on her bedroom floor, her back resting against the bed, her knuckles white as she clutched the biggest kitchen knife she could find. She was ready to kill absolutely anything that came through the bedroom door. She sat like this until her usual morning wake up alarm went off at 6am. She ignored it and continued to sit staring, smelling her attacker on the bedsheets behind her – the stench of cigarettes and cheap cologne.

...

The police station was absolutely packed with warm bodies. As with most unbearably accurate cliché's, there was no air-conditioning in the building, only a few unstable wireframe fans moving the hot air around. The only thing more insufferable than the heat was the noise. People were shouting over each other, children were screaming and crying, and what seemed like every phone in the precinct was ringing relentlessly. Tasha looked around nervously, scanning the faces of those around her for one which would fill all her future nightmares, but Vince wasn't there. In fact, there were very few police officers at all. She caught the eye of one of the other crime scene regulars making her way through the throng of people to the access door leading to the back of the station.

"Marci!" Tasha shouted over the racket, "Marci, hey!"

Marci caught a glimpse of Tasha and beckoned her over with a wave. There were deep purple bags under her eyes and she was sweating profusely. Tasha shoved through the people pressed so close together in the small space of the reception area. Shoulders and elbows jabbed into her from all directions. The air in the place was stifling, and she was sure there would be a few fainting cases before the morning was over.

"What's going on?" she asked when she finally managed to break through the crowd.

"It's not good," Marci replied before wiping her nose with the back of her hand. Her voice was thick and nasally.

"What do you mean?" Tasha asked, the fear for her own life suddenly giving way to a more homogenised panic.

Marci's eyes darted around the crowded station. She dug a tissue from her pocket and loudly blew her nose before shoving it back down.

"Look," she said, lowering her voice and bringing her face closer to Tasha's, "This flu thing's got out of hand. It's not just here, it's everywhere upstate. Some kind of fucking epidemic or something. 90% of the force didn't even show up for work today, they've either fled or died, I don't fucking know. Point is, go home, lock your doors, don't talk to anyone and wait this thing out. The less people you come into contact with, the better, okay?"

Tasha nodded, not trusting her voice.

"I gotta go," Marci said, punching a code into the pad next to the access door, "Get some supplies if you can. Water, canned food, that kinda stuff. Something you can keep for a while, until this thing blows over."

"Marci," Tasha finally managed, "Are you okay?"

Marci smiled, but it was tired and mournful. Her eyes were watery, her nose red and swollen.

"I'll be fine," she said before stepping through the door.

Tasha never saw her again.

...

Dry leaves scuttled over the parking lot of St. Bernardino Hospital in the feint breeze. Heat waves rolled off the cars still parked there, some of them empty, some of them occupied by swelling corpses trapped forever in their oven-like coffins.

Tasha rested her forehead against the chain-link fence, taking care to breathe through her mouth only. The stench was at its worst this time of day, and the scarf she'd tied around her face did little to mask it. She wiped angrily at a drop of sweat as it ran stingingly into her eye. The shade of the massive oak she was currently under shielded her from the worst of the sun's rays, but the heat coming off the tarmac in the parking lot seemed to warm her up from below through the very soles of her sneakers.

She continued to stare at the hospital entrance from the other side of the fence, not trusting herself to go any closer. She blew out a frustrated breath and kicked at the fence.

"Hey!" she shouted for what felt like the hundredth time, momentarily removing the scarf tied around her face, "Are you in there?"

But there was no answer from within, and the hospital continued to loom over her like a silent sentinel guarding some kind of portal to hell.

It had been two weeks since Marci had warned her to gather supplies and get indoors. Two weeks since her biggest concern was some crazy fucking stalker cop. Two weeks since her life had any type of semblance to sanity. Fourteen days had been all it took to completely destroy the world around her.

At first she'd stayed inside, heeding Marci's warning of not coming into contact with anyone. Tasha had no family left, no one to call and check up on, so she called the few friends she'd retained from college. None of them answered or returned her calls. That was before her cell phone reception died altogether and she couldn't call anyone even if she wanted to. The television had been no better, replaying the same bulletins over and over, warning people to stay inside even if they felt sick. Especially if they felt sick.

With each passing day it had grown quieter and quieter outside. Every now and then a car would speed past, tyres squealing. Tasha had run out of her house the last few times this happened, waving her arms madly, trying to get the driver's attention. She didn't care if they were sick, she just wanted to talk to another person, find out if they know anything about what was happening in the world. Because it was indeed the entire world which was affected by what had been labelled the "flu-demic". The last few news bulletins which were actually broadcast live said the virus had spread to every corner of the world. Major cities all over the globe were going dark – one day there were calls and texts and emails streaming out of them, the next there was simply nothing.

A week after what she'd come to think of as "Marci's premonition", she'd gone to every house in her street, knocking on doors and windows, ringing bells and calling out. But there was no one. A few times while peering through windows she caught a glimpse of a figure either lying on the couch or the floor, the skin a blueish purple, already straining to keep the gasses and fluids inside.

The stench of decay permeating from every building was bad, but the absolute quiet was worse. Every now and then she would hear a dog barking somewhere in the distance, but then all would be still again and her ears would start ringing from the very lack of sound. There had been a few fires and even a couple of explosions in the city proper, but most of them had either burned out or been doused by the recent rains.

The deep and throaty sound of thunder rumbling in the distance seemed to pantomime her thoughts. To the east the sky was a dark and ominous grey with thunderclouds racing in her direction. She looked at the hospital entrance again, willing the boy she'd seen run in there to come out.

She'd been walking to the pharmacy when she caught sight of him darting through the streets ahead of her. She called out to him, but either he didn't hear her or he didn't want her to catch up to him. He couldn't have been older than 15. Initially she'd been so startled by the sight of another person that she thought the heat was getting to her and she was hallucinating, but as the kid sprinted away he bumped into a parked SUV, setting the alarm off and a flurry of pigeons racing into the sky. Tasha ran after him, shouting for him to stop, but the few nervous glances he shot at her over his shoulder told her that only a hazmat suit would have made him comfortable enough to come close. She got it – he was scared. She was, too, in the beginning, but she'd come to the conclusion that if she hadn't gotten sick yet at this point, then she probably wasn't going to. The dead were literally lying in the street like some medieval plague procession. If she was going to catch whatever they had, she would have by now.

That morning she'd caught glimpse of the kid again, but this time she didn't just start running and shouting after him, she just watched him from afar for a while as he moved between the abandoned cars. He still looked nervous, and he was sweating in the heat. He had a backpack slung over his shoulder, much like Tasha, and from her shadowy hiding place she watched him go into the Kroger grocery store. She leaned against the side of a building, nervous and apprehensive. A part of her wanted to run into the grocery store where she could maybe corner him, but she didn't want to scare him half to death. He had bags under his eyes, not the flu-demic kind, the no-sleep kind. She wondered if he had nightmares too.

She stood waiting for him like that for what must only have been a few minutes, before he came darting out of the grocery store and down the street, back the way he'd come. She struggled to keep up with him whilst retaining a stealthy following distance. After a few blocks she couldn't keep her pursuit quiet anymore, and he seemed to double his speed when he realised she was running after him.

"Hey! Please stop! I'm not sick! I'm not going to hurt you!" she called after him desperately, but the kid just kept on running, the sound of his sneakers hitting the pavement echoing through the quiet streets.

She followed him here, to the hospital, where he burst through the double doors of the entrance and let them slam shut behind him. That was probably twenty minutes ago. She'd been standing by the fence ever since.

A hospital was a strange place to use as a hideout in normal situations. Tasha laughed to herself. What was a normal situation? She didn't know anymore. She only knew that since this whole thing started, St. Bernardino Hospital was the one place that she absolutely avoided. In her mind it was the place all of this had started, with that big stretching lawn covered in humanoid sheets baking in the heat of the day. Her imagination had turned the place into some kind of torture chamber, and all she saw when she thought about its stark white hallways were half decomposed bodies piled on top of each other, hospital beds overturned, blood smears on the walls, flickering fluorescent lights, like something from a zombie movie. Were there zombies? She wondered. Were all the dead people lining the streets and occupying the buildings going to stand up and come after her? She shook her head. Surely if that was a possibility it would have happened by now. That was the logical way to think about it, anyway, but she still cast a nervous glance at the bloated woman lying on the sidewalk a few feet away, big fat black flies lazily buzzing over her. At least the insects were flourishing.

Tasha unzipped her backpack and took recon of the items inside. Water bottle, flashlight, extra batteries, zip knife, first aid kit, lighter, a couple of breakfast bars. Her eyes lingered for a while on the last item. She struggled to suppress a shudder despite the heat. The 9mm Glock was almost completely covered in Nature's Surprise breakfast oat bars, but the weight of it was unmistakable. She didn't even know why she had it. *That's a lie,* she thought, *you know exactly why you have it, and you know you would have gotten it anyway whether the world had gone to shit or not.* She kept it in the backpack in case... In case what? She couldn't tell. She just knew that having it made her feel better somehow. She hadn't actually fired a gun in years, having never really liked the things. But desperate times and all that.

She took out the flashlight, zipped up the bag and slung it over her shoulders. She took a deep breath, through the mouth, of course. Her nose was permanently off duty to prevent her lunch from ending up on the front of her shirt. She glanced at the storm clouds approaching and calculated that she'd have probably another hour of good sunlight before she'd have to high tail it out of there. The most unexpected thing about the end of the world was how completely and utterly dark it was at night. The power had failed all over the city in stages, the last of the lights going out only a couple of days ago. For all the brilliant machines man made, they still needed maintenance. Tasha had never been afraid of the dark, but you had this way of reassessing your fears once all the lights go out forever.

She knew the hospital would be very dark inside. While the actual patient rooms had windows to let in natural light, the hallways, operating theatres and reception area would be pitch black. The layout of the place wasn't a mystery to her as she'd visited it often because of the nature of her work. But the knowledge of the floor plan did little to ease the rising trepidation she felt in her stomach.

"Okay," she said to herself, "Let's go."

The words EMERGENCY ROOM glared at her like a big red exclamation. As she walked up to the double doors she glanced at the windows looking out over the parking lot, hoping to catch a glimpse of a red baseball cap, but the sun was behind her, effectively turning all the windows into blinding mirrors. The inside of the building was surprisingly cool. Tasha stood inside the small patch of sunlight streaming in through the doors, shifting her weight from one leg to the other as she waited for her eyes to adjust to the dim light inside. The smell wasn't as bad as she expected, but she was still only in the reception area.

"Hello?" she called out nervously.

There was no reply, big surprise there.

An oppressive stillness filled the place. The air was stuffy and thick. The beam of her flashlight moved steadily over the chairs in the waiting area. She cried out loudly when it fell on the back of a man slumped over in a chair. Her hand flew to her mouth to cover the noise. Disturbing the unnatural peace in here felt like some kind of sacrilege. The man, although not bloated as the bodies outside in the sun, was obviously dead. The back of his grey shirt read "Dodgers" in big blue letters. She couldn't see his face, and for that she was grateful.

Tasha made her way through the reception area and into the hallway leading to the examination rooms. A scuttle of noise made her turn to the right. There was movement in one of the rooms down the hall. Her fight or flight instincts were kicking in hard, and her legs were itching to take her right back out into sunlight where she would be safe from the darkness and whatever was hidden in it. But the thought of the boy made her push on. The flashlight beam was shaky and unsteady. She tried to get herself under control, but the darkness and the quiet of the place seemed to press in on her from all sides. It took every ounce of strength she had to stop herself from simply trembling uncontrollably. She thought about calling out, but her voice had done that thing again where it disappeared as thoroughly as if she'd never had it. Another scuttle of noise ironed her resolve.

"Exam C" the little label on the door read. Tasha put her ear closer to the cool wood, but she couldn't hear anything else. She stood gripping the door handle for what seemed like hours before she finally convinced herself to give it a turn.

The door swung open on silent hinges, revealing the small examination room inside. The boy was half sitting half lying on the elevated examination table, his baseball cap lying on the floor. He seemed to be struggling with something one either side of his legs. His head shot up as she shone the flashlight on his face. His mouth was covered by a large piece of silver masking tape, and Tasha realised that he was struggling against restraints tying him to the table.

"Oh my god," she cried, rushing over to him, "Are you okay? Who did this to you?"

The boy continued to struggle against the restraints, his cries muffled behind the masking tape. Tasha peeled it off as gently as she could, wincing internally at the sight of the tape peeling off the top layer of skin on his dry lips.

"You have to go!" he cried frantically as soon as the tape was off.

"What?"

She was trying to undo the IV tubes that were used to tie his hands to the table, but he was struggling so much that it was hard to get a good grip on the knots. She remembered the knife in her backpack.

"You have to get out of here," the boy said pleadingly.

"Not until I've gotten you out of these," Tasha said much calmer than she felt, "What happened?"

"It's a trap," the boy whimpered.

"What do you mean?" she asked.

Who would tie up a kid in a hospital room? Who was even left to do such a thing? Her mind raced with questions, but she focused on the task of cutting him out of the tubes.

As soon as he was free he shot off the table quicker than she'd ever seen anyone move, knocking the knife out of her hand onto the floor and darting out of the room like it was on fire. Tasha stood mutely for a few seconds before running after him.

What the fuck, she thought as her flashlight caught him just before he sprinted around the corner into the reception area, *I've probably just saved his life and he thanks me by running away AGAIN?*

His silhouette was black against the light streaming in through the double doors. With a loud BANG he was through them and out into the parking lot. Tasha ran after him, her flashlight casting mad beams of light around the waiting area. It took her brain about a nanosecond to notice something she would probably have missed under any other circumstance. It must have been the adrenaline shooting through her system, heightening her observational senses to a level they'd never been before. It made her stop cold in her tracks. With a shaky hand she directed the beam to the empty chairs in the waiting area. And that's exactly what they were. Empty. The man in the Dodgers shirt was nowhere to be seen.

Her entire body went numb.

But the adrenaline was still running, and it told her to do the same. She ran for the doors and reached for them. But her fingers only managed to graze the steel handle before her arm got snatched to the side in a hard grip. Rough hands pulled her into the darkness untouched by the greying light streaming in from outside. Two arms enfolded her from behind. Her backpack and its contents dug painfully into her back as she was squeezed tightly to someone's chest.

The rough prickly texture of beard stubble grated against the side of her cheek as the man behind her pressed his mouth to her ear.

"What's the rush, honey?"

...

Stark white sheets covered everything except the bodies. The wind lifted the corners of the sheets, revealing the pristine and flawless objects below. Tasha strolled down the street, relaxed and uncaring. Each body she passed had the same face and wore the same clothes, but each was in a different stage of decomposition. She knelt down next to one and studied the face a little bit closer. The mouth and eyes were open, as if shocked by the prospect of death. She knew the facial features well. It was like looking into a mirror that could somehow show you the future. She stood up, brushed the dirt from her knees and looked around at the other bodies lying haphazardly in the street. All of them were the same. All of them were her.

Lightning flashed overhead, but instead of the sound of thunder following the explosions of light, there was a high pitched tone ascending into the clouds. It flashed again and again. She lifted her arm to shield her eyes from the light. Suddenly, from some primal depth of self-consciousness, she realised that she was afraid. In fact, she was scared to death. The sky darkened, but the lightning continued to rain down on her. She turned her head to the sound of approaching footsteps. A boy in a red baseball cap was running towards her. He was shouting something, but the high pitched tone was too loud for her to hear. Only when he got closer could she make out the word.

"Run!"

Tasha jerked awake violently, her eyes popping open in a panic. A bright flash of light assaulted her senses and she cried out. There it was again, the high pitch hum of the camera flash recharging.

"Stop!" she screamed.

The flash did not come again.

It took a while for her eyes to adjust to the darkness around her. She had no idea where she was, only that she was seated on what appeared to be a wheelchair. Her neck spasmed in pain from the way she had been slumped over for God knew how long. She tried to reach up a hand to rub it, only to feel the unrelenting steel of handcuffs stopping her short.

"I wish I didn't have to use those," an all too familiar voice said from behind her.

"Vin—Vince?" she stuttered, incredulous.

"Yes, honey," he replied, the satisfaction clearly audible in his voice.

"What—you're alive?"

"Oh yes," there was movement behind her, she tried to look around but her neck protested painfully.

"Let me out of these," she said, rattling the handcuffs against the frame of the wheelchair.

"Not quite yet," his voice was closer behind her now, "Not until I know for certain that you're going to be a good girl. And that could take weeks, maybe even months to determine."

The cold fingers of dread ran up her spine, and her bladder was dangerously close to emptying itself.

"Please," she whimpered, the sting of tears rising suddenly to her eyes.

"No, honey," he came around to stand in front of her, the big jolly blue letters on his shirt swimming in her vision.

He looked terrible. His face was covered in what looked like acne scars, but Tasha had never seen him with acne. Massive bags under his eyes and hollowed cheeks made him look about 20 years older. He'd also lost weight. But despite the change in appearance, the smell of him told her he was still a smoker, and he must have found a lifetime supply of that cheap fucking cologne he loved so much.

"You and I can finally have that dinner," he said with a smile and moved behind her again.

He pushed the wheelchair to the other side of the room. Tasha looked at the door quizzically. It was extremely familiar to her. But surely...

"Is this my house?" she stammered.

Vince laughed gleefully.

"Yes!" he said, "We can't stay at my place, the whole building fucking reeks."

He pushed her down the hallway. Candles on either side of the passage lit their way as he rolled her into the dining room. More candles were on the floor here, and on the table, which was set for two. He parked her behind one of the porcelain bowls. Cans of tinned food were stacked in the middle of the table. Vince pulled out the chair next to her and sat down, taking a napkin from the table and tucking it into the front of her shirt.

"The boy?" she asked softly as he reached for the can opener.

His hand stopped midway in the air, and a look of annoyance replaced the serene calm which had settled onto his face.

"That little punk," he spat, "You shouldn't have let him go."

His eyes flashed at her dangerously. She shrunk back into the wheelchair.

"I had to chase him down, of course," he said, the calmness returning to his face and voice, "I couldn't risk him returning the favour, now could I? Little shit joined the rest of them. He's just another dead asshole in the street now."

Tasha started to sob loudly. She couldn't help it. She wished she could join the boy as one of the dead. Anything to escape the reeking, crazy bastard sitting next to her.

"Stop crying," Vince said angrily, but her tears would not stop flowing.

Why was she left alive? Why was *he* left alive? What kind of sick cosmic joke was this?

"I said, stop crying!" the back of his hand rapped painfully across her cheek.

She stopped crying mid-sob, more out of shock than anything else.

"Now, listen" he said, struggling to keep his voice under control, "As far as I can tell, you and I are the only people left alive in this stinking shit hole. It's *fate*, honey. We were meant to be together, to start the New Earth. To repopulate it. And we can't do that when you're crying, because you're fucking ugly when you cry, and I won't have that."

He spent the next few minutes feeding her cold canned soup. At first she didn't want to eat, but a few more backhands and a busted lip made her reconsider. The soup sat unsteadily in her stomach, but she refused to be sick. She suspected that another backhand wouldn't be the only punishment for something like that.

"It's funny," he said with a chuckle once her soup was finished and he started with his own bowl, "You said, 'Not if you're the last guy on earth.' Well, here I am, honey."

He chuckled again before loudly slurping up a spoonful of soup.

"Here I am."

END

BROKEN GLASS

15

CHRIS CARR

CHAPTER ONE

"My son, keep my words and store up my commands within you," Logan said, reading from the well-worn Bible. "Keep my commands and you will live; guard my teachings as the apple of your eye. Bind them on your fingers; write them on the tablet of your heart. Say to wisdom, 'you are my sister,' and to insight 'you are my relative.'"

Logan slammed the Bible down on the counter then looked around himself. The second story loft of his farm house filled with his creations of the female form. He sculptured mini-statues, made paintings and took photographs of Cindy Eaton.

Blonde, with curly blonde hair and light brown eyes that suggested suffering.

"They will keep you from the adulterous woman, from the wayward woman with her seductive words."

Logan walked over to the coffin in the center of the loft. Looking down, he caressed the hair of the wax figure he had created.

He made Cindy look so life-like. He crafted down every detail to the beauty mark on her neck to the cleft in her chin.

Then there were the fire burns he created on one half of the figure's body.

"You're a sick man," Cindy said when she showed her the figure a half-hour earlier. "Sick."

She ran down the steps packed up her suitcase and left.

Logan stared down at the wax corpse, his perfect replication of the woman of his obsession.

"We still have more work to do," he whispered. "We're not done yet."

He slammed the coffin shut and ran down the steps, heading out of the door.

Logan leaped into his '65 Corvette convertible and sped off down the dirt road. The central California town that he lived in was so far down that it wasn't even on the map. But Logan liked it that way, he could drive as fast as he wanted.

And if he drove fast enough, he could catch her before she did something stupid.

Sure enough, about two miles down the road, he saw Cindy lugging her suitcase along.

He slowed the car down and kept pace with her as she walked, waiting for her to turn around and look his way.

"I can give you a ride," he said.

She looked back at him, shooting dagger eyes, then looked ahead and never broke her stride.

"You want a cookie, little girl?" he laughed.

"Fuck off," she said.

"You got a long walk ahead of you," he said.

"What is it about the phrase 'fuck off' that you don't understand?"

"Come on, Sweetness," Logan said. "I'm sorry. Okay? What more can I say? Call me a weirdo. Call me an asshole. Call me a jerk. But just let me drive you over to the bus depot. You're going to ruin those shoes that I bought you."

"I'm breaking them in," she said.

"You won't make it there in time," Logan said. "Only bus leaves at 3 o'clock. You have less than a half-hour."

Cindy gripped the handles around her suitcase and picked up her pace.

"Come on," he said. "You won't make it in time and then you'll be another woman all dressed up with no place to go."

Cindy looked at her watched then stopped in place.

"You are a fucking asshole."

"Guilty as charged," he said. "But I'm an apologetic asshole."

Cindy looked back down the empty road. "If I go with you-"

Logan opened his driver side door.

"Stop," she said. "If I go with you we are going straight to the bus depot. No turning the car around. No talking me out of this."

Logan put up his hands in appeasement.

"Okay."

"I'm not playing."

Logan nodded his head and reached over to open the passenger side door.

"Neither am I," he whispered under his breath as Cindy ran around the front of the car to get in his vehicle.

Spotting himself in the rear view mirror, Logan knew he had looked at least a decade older than his calendar age. Everything about his face was long, from the stretch of forehead between his thin brown hair and fading brown eyebrows, to the nose that ran from his blood shot eyes to his scowling lips, to the lines that grooved the skin under his eyes across his face. His skin was the color of rotten buttermilk, which his choice of gray t-shirts and blue jeans only emphasized.

Still, Cindy got into the car, beautiful on the surface but seeing a lot of herself in the melancholy that was Logan Metcalf.

CHAPTER TWO

The two drove in silence down the long road for about two miles. Logan kept looking at Cindy, waiting for some kind of opening.

She reached over and turned on the radio dial.

"Sorry sunshine," he said. "I haven't fixed that yet."

Instead, she looked through her purse then out the back window. In the distance, she saw the Greyhound bus gaining speed on the Corvette.

"There's my bus," she said.

"It won't pick you up in the middle of the road."

Logan reached over and ran his fingers through her hair. She pushed his hand away.

"Take it easy," he said. "You a piece of hay in there."

Cindy looked over at him and rolled her eyes.

"I can't wait to sit in a salon," she said. "Get my hair done. Get a manicure. Pedicure. Then eat out at a real restaurant. Not a diner. And then go to a 3-D movie. I heard those are great. Or maybe I'll just sit at a cafe and people watch. Will be nice to see crowds of people again. Jesus."

"I hate crowds," Logan said. "Especially ones with people."

"Or maybe just hang out in a dive bar," she said. "Like when I was in college. Where the air is just fresh with possibilities. You can smell the perfume, cotton and shampooed hair, burning tobacco and pot. Beer and lust."

"You need to just start writing again."

The bus passed the Corvette on the left hand side of the road.

Logan slowed his car down.

"You're not going slow on purpose are you?"

"Why would I want to do that?"

"Fuck, Logan, you are going to make me miss the bus!"

"Am I?" Logan turned to her with a smug smile. He turned the steering wheel to his left, making a sharp turn off the road and into some grass land.

"Logan!"

He put the car in reverse and headed back down the road in the opposite direction.

"I don't believe this," she said. "You're such a liar! Stop the fucking car. Stop!"

"Your wish," Logan slammed on the brakes and Cindy pitched forward hitting her head on the dashboard. "Is my command."

Logan pushed his door open and marched over to the passenger side. He ripped the door open and grabbed Cindy, throwing her to the ground.

"Go on! Get the fuck outta here. Get out of my line of vision. Go back to where you came from."

"Fucking asshole!" Cindy screamed, hitting him in the face with her purse. "Fuck you. And your art. You're not an artist. You're just a psycho!"

Logan went back into his car and started it up again.

Cindy started walking back to the road, giving him the middle finger.

Then Logan started after her, following her with the car, speeding up as she started to run.

"Go bitch!" he screamed as he picked up speed. "Run bitch run!"

Cindy turned around and sprinted away as fast as she could. She could feel the Corvette hot on her heels.

Then she pitched forward as she tripped on rock, hitting her head on the gravel hard.

Logan hit the brakes on the Corvette. He sprang out of his car, running over to Cindy now laying face first in the dirt. He knelt down and rolled her over, caressing her face.

She's crying.

"I'm so sorry," he said. "Why do we keep doing this to each other? This can't keep happening."

Cindy shook her head in response, slipping in and out of consciousness.

"I'm so sorry," he kissed her lips. "For how I make you feel sometimes. I'll change. I promise. I'll change for you."

She pressed her head against his chest as he held her tight.

"You're like the morning breeze," he said. "Touching you is like kissing an angel."

Cindy began to sob then passed out.

The sun had come down by the time the reached the farm house.

Logan carried the sleeping Cindy back into the home, carrying her all the way into his bedroom.

"Sleep it off," Logan whispered as he laid Cindy onto the mattress "It has all been a bad dream."

Logan sighed deep as he looked down at the unconscious Cindy. He then walked over to the closet next to the bed and took out a pink dress with the store's plastic wrap still around it.

"This'll work," he said, laying the dress her prone body. "This will work just right."

Cindy took a deep breath and rolled over.

"Rest up, Sleeping Beauty," Logan stepped out of the bedroom and closed the door behind himself.

Logan sponged down the hood of the '65 Ford Mustang in his garage. The car had belonged to his father over forty years ago and now he had almost completely restored the vehicle. Old cars were his father's hobby and he shared the same affinity for the old Mustangs and Chevys.

Out of the corner of his eye, he saw the young man come into the lot outside the garage. He pretended not to see him at first, waiting to see what the drifter would do.

The man looked inside the rusted '56 Chevy, his grandfather's old car that he fully restored.

Logan set down his sponge and began walking toward the intruder.

"Hey asshole," he said. "That piece of tin is over sixty years old. Not really ideal for a getaway car."

The drifter turned around and held up a long steel pipe that he had hidden under his shirt. He waved the weapon with menace at Logan.

Logan sighed hard and shook his head as if disappointment. He reached into his pocket and took out a one hundred dollar bill, holding it up to the young man.

"You looking to just rip someone off or are you looking for work?"

The drifter let the pipe down to his side, eyeballing the money. He walked forward and took hold of the bill.

Logan pulled his hand back, ripping off his end of the one hundred dollar bill.

"You look just like him," Logan said, staring at the young drifter with incredulity.

The young man said nothing, just cocked his head at Logan.

"Follow me," Logan said, turning his back on the drifter and leading him further into the shed.

The drifter stood in place, not moving.

Logan turned back around. "Do you want to earn some money or not?"

The drifter followed as Logan turned on another light, revealing his work station at the rear of the garage. A lathe and numerous art palettes laid about.

Logan squinted his eyes at the young man, seeing the scratches on his face. "The hell happened to you?"

"Been running," he said, scanning Logan up and down with eyes that harbored a lifelong grudge against the world. "Through the woods."

Logan made a twirling motion with his fingers, wanting the man to spin around. "Let me take a look at you."

"If you-"

"I don't bite," Logan said as he pushed aside a lock of the man's hair from his eyes.

The drifter pushed away Logan's hand.

"Take it easy, sunshine," Logan said.

"If you're a fag-"

"I have a job for you," Logan laughed.

"I just need a place to crash for the night."

"You got three hots and a cot plus some cash. How's that sound?"

"In exchange for what?"

"Your ass-"

The drifter turned around and started walking. "Faggot ass-"

"I'm kidding," Logan laughed. "Come on, back. Come on, I couldn't resist. No. What I need from you is to have you model for me. I'm a photographer. Painter. Sculptor. Artist."

Logan waved his arms around work station as Terry looked at all of the eclectic art.

"I don't do anything gay," the young man said.

Logan took out his camera from the desk and focused on Terry through the lens. "Don't worry, Sunshine," he said laughing.

CHAPTER THREE

Cindy woke up to faint sounds coming from the kitchen. She thought she heard voices but wrote it off to Logan talking to himself again. She got up and felt woozy, as she walked over to her make-up desk.

"Fucking asshole," Cindy said, looking at the bump on her forehead in the mirror. "Dumb fucking creep."

Cindy didn't remember how she got in the bed. The last thing she remembered was running away from the Corvette.

She looked at the unmade bed and felt like going back to sleep until she again heard voices coming from the kitchen. One of them didn't sound like Logan.

"Damn, dude," Logan said. "You're eating like you just ended a hunger strike."

Cindy opened her bedroom door, stepped down the hall and -

"Boo!" Logan said, greeted her just as she walked into the kitchen. "Shit!"

"We have company," he said, nodding his head over at the drifter sitting at the table.

Cindy saw the young man scarfing down Logan's charred hash browns and sausage. He took a big gulp of orange juice and belched as she stepped inside.

His manners aside, she thought he was the most handsome man she had ever seen.

"Terry," Logan said. "This is Cindy. You'll be working together."

The young man didn't look up. He continued to stuff the hash browns into his mouth as if the plate were about to be taken away.

"Hey," Cindy said.

The man finally looked up. She gasped at the color of his slate blue eyes, feeling as if she were looking at a different breed of human being.

He nodded his head at Cindy and returned his attention to the breakfast Logan prepared for him.

"People thought my art was pretentious," Logan said as led Terry back into his shed. "So I like the fact you don't come from that world. You'll be able to see things with a fresh point of view unlike so many of those college pukes I've worked with in the past."

The young man watched as Logan opened a binder filled with old newspaper articles and pictures. Sifting through the pages, Logan took out the last one, handing the paper to Terry.

"What's this?" Terry asked, looking down on the caption that read "Couple Crashes To Death."

"With persuasive words she led him astray," Logan said. "She seduced him with her smooth talk. Proverbs 7:21."

Terry looked back at the photo in the newspaper article. The picture showed a smashed up, burned out automobile.

"Okay," he said, still not understanding.

"It is the inspiration for my new sculpture," Logan said. "My mother had ran away with this young drifter. Looked like you, a bit. Good looking, muscular guy. She left my Dad for him. Only they didn't get far. They drove into a wall and burned to death."

"Sorry," Terry said.

"It was a long time ago," Logan said. "Now I have to use that pain. Use that memory and create art. If I can do that, then that haunting memory becomes a gift. A gift from the Gods."

Logan took the article away from Terry and placed it back into his binder.

"Come on," he said, leading Terry back into the garage and to the white Mustang.

"Was my Dad's old car," he said, knocking on the convertible top. "Take the other end, will you?"

The two men stood at opposite ends of the convertible top and lifted it off the car.

"Right on," Logan said, handing a bucket of soap water to Terry. "Make this baby shine, okay? I want it looking slicker than baby shit."

Logan looked out the garage window and saw Cindy walking toward the shed with two glasses of lemonade.

"You'll find some extra soap in the cabinets over there," Logan said, stepping out of the garage to avoid Cindy. "I'll be back with some wax."

Cindy entered the garage, her eyes shifting left and right.

"Where is he?" she asked, almost in a whisper.

Terry said nothing, pointing to the direction where Logan left.

"I brought you guys some lemonade," she said, laying the glasses on the hood. . "It is hot as heck in here."

Terry ignored the offer and continued to wipe down the Mustang.

"What a pig sty," Cindy said, looking around the garage. "I swear these artists are worse than farm animals. Matter of fact, I think that would be an insult to farm animals."

"This is a step up for me," Terry said, finally taking one of the lemonade glasses and taking a sip.

"Where are you from?"

"Ah, you know how it is. Here, there, and nowhere."

"Sounds lonely," Cindy said, moving closer to him. "Where are your people from?"

"My people?"

"I'm originally from Fernley," Cindy said. "We called it Ferntucky. Bunch of people talking with Southern accents who live in friggin' Nevada. If you fart while you're driving you'll miss it. Both of my folks are dead but I have an older brother. I should go visit him out there. How about you?"

Terry put the glass of lemonade down. He looked around to make sure Logan was out of ear shot, still uncomfortable that Cindy would be taking such an interest in him.

"Yeah, you, I'm talking to you. Where are you headed?"

"South," he said. "I want to go to Los Angeles."

"I love L.A.," she said. "Palm trees. The beach. God, that sounds fantastic."

She took the glass of lemonade off the hood and rubbed her forehead with it.

The drifter looked her up and down, her tight white blouse leaving nothing to the imagination.

Cindy returned the stare, looking deep into the drifter's eyes as if trying to communicate her attraction without saying a word. She noticed that he didn't have eyes that suggested intelligence as much as an undeniable presence.

"I should give Logan his lemonade," she said, leaving the shed.

CHAPTER FOUR

"Closer," Logan said, commanding his two models. "Stick your arms out and move them closer. Good."

Both Cindy and Terry lay face first on the ground. Cindy wore the retro pink dress while Terry wore a greasy t-shirt and jeans.

They both laid there, facing one another in a fake death scene.

"Okay," Logan said, snapping some pictures while pouring more broken candy glass round them. "Now don't move. Don't even breathe!"

"It only gets worse," Cindy said with humor. "He gets like this all the time. Gets a vision in his head and it goes on for hours and days on end. He calls it inspiration. I call it schizophrenia."

"I didn't know modeling would be this hard."

"It isn't," Cindy said. "It's Logan that's hard."

"This is insane," Logan said, giddy with excitement. "It is as if I've been given a gift. You two look perfect for one another. The perfect scene."

Logan studied the scene again, moving Terry's arm closer to Cindy. Terry pulled his arm back.

"I said don't move," Logan said, readjusting.

Terry looked at Cindy and the woman rolled her eyes.

Logan circled around the couple again, taking more still pictures. Then he adjusted the light so the broken glass sparkled back to his camera lens.

"This will be my finest work," he said. "All of that time spent creating will culminate with this masterpiece. It will have everything. Lust. Betrayal. Death."

He took a couple more shots and the camera bulb flashed across the shed, lighting the place up as if he were a crime scene photographer.

"This screams something personal," Logan said. "All of my other work as been nothing compared to this. Empty. Lifeless. Inert. Up until now."

He stood up both Cindy and Terry and shot one last picture.

"I can feel them," he said. "My mother and her lover. I can touch them. I can hear her voice. Okay. Done."

Cindy sprang up and dusted herself off.

"Well, that was fun," she said her voice having more than a trace of sarcasm.

Logan watched as Cindy walked in the back room and slipped out of the dress, putting on her blouse.

The drifter took out a piece of bubble gum from his blue jean pocket and snapped it into his mouth.

"I was seven years old," Logan said, looking through his camera at his shots. "My father and I were following them. Then we saw them disappear off the road and crash. We got out of the car and I ran over to edge of the road. I don't know why my father took me with him.

Why he wanted me to see it. I never saw so much broken glass in my life. It was everywhere. Then the car burst into flames. I just saw the fire below and that is when I got interested in photography. I bought a camera with my savings and spent days just looking through the lens. Then something weird happened. I realized I wasn't holding a camera. I was holding my father's eyes."

"Logan," Cindy poked her head back into the shed. "I'm going to be out by the pond."

Logan nodded his head as he watched Cindy walk past the front window.

"Women," he said. "So damn sweet when you first meet them. Then it changes. It changes for the worst always. It just varies in degrees. And with that one"

Logan shook his head in disgust.

"She doesn't seem so bad," Terry said, following Logan's eye line as he watched Cindy.

"Go find out for yourself," Logan laughed. "Keep an eye on her for me, okay? We have a few more shots to go."

Terry looked out the front window, watching as Cindy ran her fingers through her hair and stretched out. The sun hitting her blouse from behind, showing off her curvaceous figure.

"In the Greek myths," Logan said. "Actaeon was a hunter who stumbled upon Diana bathing in a sacred pool. For stealing a glance at her divine body, the hunter was transformed into a deer and then ripped apart by his own dogs."

"What's that supposed to mean?"

"Go and find out," Logan said, stepping away from the young drifter.

CHAPTER FIVE

Cindy leaned back against the tree with her eyes closed, absorbing the rays of sun.

Terry stepped in front of her, casting a shadow above her.

She opened one eye and looked up at the man, her face creasing in to a lustful smile.

"Nothing feels better than sunshine," Cindy said, reaching over and holding up a bottle of scotch. "Well, almost nothing."

"It's really beautiful out here," Terry said, taking the bottle of liquor. "Hot but beautiful."

"Sit down. Let's talk."

Terry looked back at the garage, wanting to see if Logan was still watching. He saw nothing through the front glass window then he sat down.

"You look like you have something on your mind," she said.

"I don't know if it is my place to say," he said, drinking from the bottle before handing it back to Cindy. The Scotch flared on his tongue.

"Well, you may as well say it anyway."

"If you hate him so much, why do you stay?" Terry asked.

"Good question," Cindy said. "There are good questions and stupid ones. But that's a good one."

"You're smart," he said. "And pretty. Isn't there anywhere else you can go?"

"Pretty doesn't last," Cindy said, looking up at the sky.

"What did you do before you came here?"

"I was a performance poet," Cindy smiled at the memory. "Played in Reno of all places. Not exactly a place where expect to experience high art. Bu I had a five piece rock band behind me. Guitars, keyboards, bass, drums and my poetry and singing."

"You were a singer?"

"A lousy one," she said. "But I could write. I should have found someone with some talent that could front a band. Then be the producer or something. I wrote songs about spending holidays alone. Taking long walks alone."

"Sounds depressing."

"I call it recreational depression," she said. "That is what I saw in Logan. He was obviously disturbed but there was something about him. He gave off these cues, you know, really subtle at first, that he wasn't on the same road as anyone I'd ever met."

"I never met an artist before," Tyler said.

"What did you want to be when you grew up?"

"A magician."

"Why?"

"So I could disappear."

The two said nothing for a few moments until Cindy looked up at the sky and closed her eyes.

"God, this is the time of day I hate the most."

"Why?"

"Sundown," Cindy said. "I hate the night. Feels like I'm being closed in. Like someone is shutting the coffin door over my dead body."

"Sorry to hear that."

Cindy turned and looked at Terry with the saddest eyes he'd ever seen. "Let's run away."

"What?"

"We can run away together," she said. "It doesn't matter where. We'll figure it out."

"I've got nothing," he said. "I can't..I can't provide for you...The way he can."

"Is that what your momma told you?"

"What?"

"Guys who think that way always have mothers who bad talked their fathers. Like they didn't do enough. So the son inherits the bad vibes."

"It ain't like that."

"So come with me," Cindy said, standing up and wiping the grass off her buttocks. "We'll figure it out."

Logan watched from the window as Cindy led the young man into the barn.

Cindy opened the barn door and then slammed it shut when Terry entered.

She pulled the latch down, locking them in.

"What are you doing?" he asked.

She unbuttoned her blouse and threw it on the haystack, revealing her ample bosom held up by a white lace bra.

Terry mouth gaped as he couldn't help but marvel at her ivory white flesh in stark contrast to the darkness of their surroundings.

"Come closer," she said, smiling at his hesitation. "Think about it. We can steal the Mustang and ditch it as soon as we're far away. Just the two of us. A fresh start. Doesn't that sound romantic?"

Cindy pressed up against the drifter. She took his hand and let him feel her breasts.

"Jesus," he muttered, kneading the softness of her bosom.

Cindy moaned as she felt the roughness of his hands that felt like padded leather gloves.

"God, you're beautiful," he whispered.

She ripped off his shirt to reveal a rudely muscled bare torso and broad shoulders.

"The feeling is mutual," she said. "I know you're younger than me. Don't let that stop you. Don't be shy. Do the things that you've always dreamed about."

Terry nodded, looking at her breasts as if they were the first pair he had ever seen.

Cindy started to unbuckle his pants. "These should have been off by now," she said.

Terry began kissing Cindy's neck. Softly at first then and losing himself in his own lust, running his tongue up and down her neck.

Logan studied both of the wax figures of Terry and Cindy on the display. He blew off the excess saw dust off the replica of Terry's head.

"My finest work," he said. "My finest work ever."

He then placed the bodies closer together. He tossed some gasoline over the figures before attaching the blowtorch to his back and pulling the release button. The flames ignited the display, lighting up Logan's face. He then set down his blowtorch and began snapping pictures with the camera, weary about getting too close to the fire.

Logan watched as the legs of Cindy's figure began to melt into a dark, slug-like shape. He quickly snapped pictures of that happening before turning to Terry's figure.

Through the lens, he watched Terry's wax face melted into a dark viscosity as the flames worked there way up, the heat extending the features of his face, stretching and distorting them in strange ways.

He removed the blowtorch from the counter and sprayed more flames onto Cindy's face. Her head then began to melt, her facial expression looking like that of a drowning woman just about to go under for the last time and knowing it.

Logan smiled as he snapped off shot after shot.

"I want you to fuck me hard," Cindy whispered as she laid back down on the haystack. "Pull down my pants. Unhook my bra. Slid my panties down to my ankles."

Terry obeyed, entering her womanhood.

"Pound me," she said.

Terry began thrusting inside her, giving in to her unashamed carnality. He tensed and tightened his hips, cupping his hands around her shoulders.

She screamed and dug her nails into his back, then she pushed him back and mounted him, her hips gyrating.

"I've been so lonely," she whispered as he began caressing her breasts. "I've been waiting for you. Been waiting for you for so long."

Cindy reached down over and squeezed his balls, bringing him to a loud and thunderous climax.

He came hard and she leaned forward into him, resting her head on his chest.

"Are you going to take me with you?"

"I am not going anywhere without you by my side," he said, lust pouring out of him like a fever, whatever resistance he had toward her now incinerated by her passion.

They sat back in a lover's embrace on the haystack., laying there for the better part of an hour. The hay was soft. Terry's eyes began to droop.

"Terry!"

They both flinched as they heard Logan's voice.

Terry looked at Cindy for her to give him a cue as to what the proper response should be.

"See what he wants," she said.

He sprang up and put on his blue jeans, his underwear still somewhere in the haystack.

CHAPTER SIX

"Where have you been, boy?" Logan asked from the second story of the loft. "Been looking for you everywhere."

"Smells like something's burning," Terry said, noticing the smoke behind Logan.

"The hell were you? I didn't say go and make hay with that little whore."

Terry balled up his fists and tightened his jaws.

"Don't stand there with your jaws clenched up," Logan said. "Come on up."

Terry came up the steps, stopping at the top of the wooden stairwell.

"I don't bite," Logan said, motioning for Terry to come closer.

"Don't call her a little whore," Terry said.

"With persuasive words she led him astray," Logan said. "She seduced him with her smooth talk."

"The hell you talking about?"

"All at once he followed her, like an ox going to the slaughter, like a deer stepping into a noose, till an arrow pierces his liver, like a bird darting into a snare, little knowing it will cost him his life."

"You're a religious kook."

"My father was a pastor," he said. "We had two phones in the house. Mom hadn't been home for awhile. I was waiting for her to call home Call to tell me that everything was okay. Then finally the phone rang and Dad took the call in the bathroom. I went to listen on the other end, in the living room. She told my Dad she slept with the drifter. This asshole from the church that my Dad hired to help paint the church. Mom started to cry. Ashamed. Said she was running away with the mother fucker. I hung up and my Dad heard the click. I walked over and he looked at me, his face filled with darkness. Then he started pacing around the living room, the entire house felt like a cage."

"Doesn't justify treating her the way you do. She's not your mom."

"No, she isn't" Logan said as he reached into Terry's hair and pulled out a piece of hay. "She's just a woman who has weakness for drifters like you. Strays. Guys who are just meandering through life. Guys who have defects that isolate themselves from the rest of society. Then she can come alone and make everything okay. Design you to her own specifics."

"Doesn't make her a whore."

"Makes her a woman who can't be trusted," he said. "Hook up with her and you'll find her naked in bed with another man so fast it will make your head spin. Shit, you've never been with a woman like Cindy. I can just by looking at you."

Terry shook his head and smirked. "If she cheats on you why do you stay?"

"It makes me want her more," Logan said.

"You're a sick man. One of these religious nuts that talks in riddles but really doesn't know what the hell he's talking about."

"Look at you. You don't even see yourself. Let me guess, she gave you the old damsel in distress routine? Or maybe the romantic 'let's run away together', like you guys are sixteen years old or something."

"Shut the fuck up," Terry said, reaching out to grab Logan by the shirt but the artist caught his wrist then pushed him back.

"How did I know she was going to do that?" Logan asked. "She said 'I've been waiting for you. Let's run away to Los Angeles. See the palm trees. The beach.' Right? I know all about it, Terry. Proverbs 8:27, her house is a highway to the grave, leading down to the chambers of death!"

Logan walked over and opened the coffin.

Terry gasped as he looked inside and saw Cindy's likeness.

"Picasso said that all art is a lie that tells the truth," Logan said, pointing down at Cindy's figure. "Do you believe me now?"

Terry's heart pounded in his ears. His tongue dead in his mouth, he could only nod his head.

"Now get this little whore out of our lives, son," Logan threw the keys of the Mustang at Terry.

CHAPTER SEVEN

Cindy entered the dark garage with her coat and suitcase.

"Terry?" she whispered.

Terry stepped down the stairs, not making a sound until he hit the bottom step creaked.

"Terry? Is that you?"

The young man cloaked himself in the dark, sliding inside the Mustang and turning on the engine. The lights flashed on, startling Cindy.

"Terry! Terry!"

"An adulterous generation seeketh after a sign," Logan cried out, his blow torch in hand. "Leading down to the chambers of death."

Cindy backed toward the garage wall, frightened as Terry revved the engine.

"Terry!" she said. "Don't do this."

With the car in park, he pressed on the gas again. The Mustang rumbled.

Terry laughed.

Cindy ran toward the car and got into the passenger side. She grabbed Terry's shirt and pulled him close.

"Kiss me," she said.

"I can't."

"We can put all of this in the rear view mirror! Everything about bad about your life. My life. We can leave it all behind now."

She kissed him hard on the lips. Terry resisted.

"Forget about him," she said. "You can be with me. We can live. Or you can be with him and be dead. Become part of the blackness. Part of his sick world."

Terry said nothing as Cindy kissed him again.

"We can live," she said. "We can run away together."

"Whore!" Logan slammed his fist on the hood of the Mustang.

Terry didn't argue anymore. He obeyed the woman's commands.

Terry hit the gas and the Mustang plowed through the wall of the barn as Logan leapt out of the way.

It skidded down the gravel road, weaving around as Tyler lost control of the wheel.

Logan leapt onto the hood, spraying the windshield in flames with the blow torch. "You ain't leaving me!"

Blinded by the fire, both Terry and Cindy lowered their heads as the Mustang sped headlong into the farmhouse wall.

The gas tank of the car ignited and blew upon impact.

Engulfed in flames, the screams of all three tortured souls echoed into the night.

SCALPED

JEFF VAN ZANT

Chapter One

Sliding out from under the desk, Tom Henderson gave the new wiring to the computers one last look over, and then stood up slowly. Didn't want to bang his head against the edge of the table and pass out. Again. No reason to go through that embarrassment again.

He brushed the dust off the front of his jeans and then smiled at the office manager while he resettled his glasses on his face. She was a beauty. Sasha Verdun was an Asian beauty with dark skin and slanted almond eyes. Her hair was cut close to the curve of her head except for a long, thinly braided tail. Her purple dress left very little to the imagination, including the fact that Sasha preferred thongs.

Tom was kind of partial to them himself.

"All done," he said, straightening the collar of his checkered shirt. He wasn't the typical geek, or at least he liked to think so. Thin but athletic, his eyes were a deep blue and his smile had been described as "delicious" by one former girlfriend. Not that he'd had many, but the fact was he was intelligent and funny even if most people only saw him as the computer nerd who understood the difference between ASP and ISP. He was even moderately rich, because the IT field paid better than people realized and up to now he'd only had himself to spend money on.

"Good," she told him in that lightly-accented way of hers. She smiled at him, and oh damn how he wished that smile was for more than just him being the IT guy, somebody she had to be polite to, somebody she only called when the computer needed a new power source or she'd forgotten her password.

Ifucku. He had it memorized.

His pants began to get tighter as he stood there, and he knew it was time to go. Sasha was a wild thing, and if he could just find a way to make her see that he liked to be wild as much as the next guy, then he knew they could have a good time. As it was, she was already checking her watch and wondering how much longer she was going to have to stand here talking with Tom the guy from IT.

He smiled back, letting his fantasies make his manhood twinge just one more time, and then he turned away to leave. He could almost hear her sigh in relief that he was going. He picked up his backpack of tools and devices as he left. Someday he'd show her that he was a man worthy of taking into her bed...er, life. Into her life, he meant.

The executive offices of Jansen and Howe took up the entire fourth floor of this highrise office building. When he got to the front of the suite, where elevators waited to take him back to his cubicle on the second floor, he smiled at Audrey Simms at her secretary's desk. She smiled back shyly. Her dark brown dress hid her curves, and her shapely legs, just like her long and curly hair hid the contours of her cheeks. He'd seen her lift that dress to adjust her pantyhose on her creamy white legs, though, and he'd seen the tattoo that she had inked at the small of her back. Audrey was a bad girl. He'd be willing to put money down on that.

Only, she was afraid to show it to people. She waved to him but then quickly put her head down again, typing away at her computer screen, avoiding eye contact. Tom was willing to bet that if he could get Audrey alone, just the two of them, then he'd be able to coax her out of her shell. He'd be able to experience the inner woman she kept caged inside. Only, she wouldn't give him the time of day. Just like Sasha. Both women looked at him and only saw a geek who was here to do a job.

Well, he was more of a man than either of them would ever know. He ground his teeth together as he stepped onto the elevator and then watched the doors slowly close off his view of Audrey. Her eyes flicked up at him just before they shut completely, and he was about to say something, but then the doors closed and the elevator moved and he was out of luck.

That was the way things went for him. He was a man looking for love, but he was never able to find it. Either the girls ignored him, or they laughed in his face, or they gave him some half-baked excuse about why they couldn't date Tom Henderson. He knew he wasn't much to look at, but if he could only get them to see him...

Well. They weren't going to look at him unless something changed. He would have to make it change somehow.

Only, he had no idea how to make that happen.

He looked up when the elevator doors dinged open. He was in the lobby. First floor, not second. He looked at the buttons on the elevator. The number two was still lit up from where he had pushed it, but for some reason the damned thing had brought him all the way down to the spacious entry area. Security guards at their station between the doors to the street and the elevators turned around to look at him. Not wanting to look stupider than he already did, Tom got off the elevator here like that had been the plan all along.

"Hey, buddy," one of the guards called to him. "1975 called. It wants its shirt back."

The other guard laughed so hard coffee spit out the corner of his mouth. Tom bent his head and balled his fists. Then he turned on his heel and made a beeline out the front doors, down the limestone steps, and tuned up the sidewalk in a random direction. He imagined he could still hear the laughter behind him.

Well, that was just great. That was exactly the way the whole day was going. He decided he needed a breather anyway. He didn't usually leave the office until lunchtime but as far as anyone was concerned he was still up on the fourth floor fixing a computer issue, so he had some time to walk and clear his thoughts.

Only, his thoughts didn't want to be cleared. He kept thinking about Sasha's tight body, and Audrey's repressed sexual desires, and soon it was hard to walk straight and keep his toolkit strategically placed to hide the bulge in his pants. There had to be something he could do to get one of the two women to notice him. Didn't there?

"Come on, Tom," he mumbled to himself. "You're a smart guy. Figure it out, damn it."

"Excuse me, sir," an old woman said to him. "Were you talking to me?"

She was sitting in a rocking chair in the alcove of her shop, smoking a pipe of all things. A colorful piece of cloth held back her long gray hair. The sun had dried her skin to the color and texture of leather and Tom had to wonder if she didn't spend all day, every day, right here on the street talking to passersby. Her dress and shawl were as colorful as her headpiece and he knew what she was, and what her business would be selling, before he even caught sight of the name spelled out in gold stick-on letters in the window.

Madame Toufou, Teller of Truths.

"You're a fortune teller," he blurted out. He wasn't trying to be rude, but it still surprised him that anyone believed in this stuff in a society marked by amazing scientific discoveries and technologies. It was all right, he supposed, if it was just for fun.

"Ah, I am more than a fortune teller," Madame Toufou told him with a grin that showed a missing front tooth. Her voice was raspy and accented with Italian. "I am the seer of the future. I am the finder of truths. For an extra few dollars, I even dabble in love spells to attract the fairer sex."

She cackled at that, and Tom had to wonder if she'd ever been considered one of the faire sex by a man in her youth. Then again, she was a woman, and she did understand these things better than he would. He was here, and he had a few minutes to spare...

And who knew? It might be fun.

She saw his decision on his face. "All right, then! Come with me, young man. Come into Madame Toufou's domain."

She levered herself up from her chair, standing stoop shouldered and leaning heavily on a stout wooden cane. Then she led him inside the shop.

It took a moment for his eyes to adjust in the gloom. Candles were the only light, burning on shelves and side tables, illuminating stacks of books and display cases full of crystals and glass orbs for sale. At the back of the small room there was a round table set up with a deep purple cloth hanging over it. On top, a large crystal ball sat in place on a round wooden disc. Madame Toufou sat in one chair on the far side of the table. With the stem of her pipe, she motioned or Tom to take the other chair.

"This is a little theatrical, isn't it?" he asked her as he sat himself down.

"Shh," she ordered. "I am already reading your wants and desires."

She held her hands up in the air, swinging the fingers on her one hand and the pipe in the other. Eyes half closed, she murmured an incantation of some kind.

Then she stopped, and stared directly at him.

"You wish the affections of two women." Her voice was strong and certain as she said it. "One is tall and dark. Asian, I think. She has a way about he that makes you want to take her forcefully and spend out all of you desires on her until she lies quivering in your arms, begging for more."

Tom gaped. Madame Toufou was describing Sasha. "How did you—?"

"Quiet," she snapped. "Do not interrupt. The second is a woman who hides her sexual nature behind a mask of inhibition. She is beautiful but doesn't know to show it. This one makes you want to draw her out a little at a time until she comes pouring over you like a tidal wave that can not stop. You wish to make her burn with passion for you."

Audrey. That was a perfect description of Audrey. "Uh. Yes. Yes, there are two women like that, in my office. I've been trying to meet them."

"Shush! You will not speak except to answer my question. Which one do you desire most?"

Her hands began to move again in time to a music only she could hear.

Which one? Tom had no idea how to answer that. He'd lusted after both of them for a very long time. Which one?

"I don't know," he finally said.

"You must choose." Madame Toufou began chanting again, murmuring and waving her hands, leaning her head back, her eyes lidding over. "Choose."

"I can't. I mean, either of them, I guess..."

"Which one?"

"I don't know what to say. Uh, I don't know..."

"Choose!"

"I don't know...Sasha...no, wait...Audrey...no..."

"You must choose!" Her chanting grew louder, and louder still. "Choose!"

"Audrey! No, Sasha. Definitely Sasha...no..."

"Choose now! Now!"

"Either of them. No, wait. Both of them! I want both of them!"

Madame Toufou rushed her hands together over her head, and the sound of them meeting was impossibly loud. Like a thunderclap. The force of it pushed Tom's chair back against the floor and left his ears ringing. He found he was panting, as if he'd just run a mile. The whole experience left him shaking.

What had he just done?

"That," Madame Toufou said as she went back to puffing on her pipe, "will be two hundred dollars. I accept credit cards, I you prefer."

Then she smiled at him, like she'd just done him the biggest favor of his life...or played the biggest practical joke in history.

Chapter Two

Laying on his couch made his head stop pounding. A cold towel over his eyes helped, too. His boss hadn't sounded happy when he'd called in for a sick day but he hadn't taken any time off in two years. They didn't have much choice but to say okay.

So it was time to rest and recuperate. Fun or not, the fortune teller had taken a seriously whacked out direction. He needed the rest.

Then the doorbell rang, and his idea of taking a nap on the couch was going to have to wait.

What stung the most, he thought to himself, is how he'd paid over the two hundred dollars by using his debit card without even hesitating. Like she'd done him some big favor by pointing out that he had two hot women in his life who could be his but weren't, and he had no one else to fill that void. So, thanks a lot Madame Nutjob, but next time he wanted to be screwed over he'd just bend over and—

When he opened the door, Sasha was standing there.

She looked at him with those big, brown eyes of hers and bit her lower lip as she drank him in with her gaze. "Um, hello Tom. I hope I'm not disturbing you?"

Her voice was soft and smoky, and her eyes would not stop fidgeting over his body, snagging on his hips and his wiry chest and his...man parts. He'd changed out of his plaid collared shirt as soon as he got home, into a more comfortable t-shirt and now, considering who it was that had rang his doorbell, he was glad he had. Even if the shirt had the image of the TARDIS on it made from Doctor Who slogans. It was obviously working for her.

"Hey, Sasha." He felt oddly at ease talking to her, which was completely out of character for him. Maybe it was because he was at home, on his own turf, and not seeing her at the office. Or heck, maybe it was the spell that Madame Mumbo Jumbo had cast. Whatever. He didn't care. As long as he felt so much in control, so damned masculine, he was going to use it to his advantage. "You want to come in?"

"Uh-huh," she murmured, nodding her head and already easing past him in a way that made her body brush against his. Her breasts slid over his shoulder and sent heat coursing through him. "I want you to take a look at my laptop. They said you'd gone home though so I came here...I hope that's all right."

She lowered her head and looked at him through her lashes. Tom closed the door behind him, staring at Sasha the whole time. Was this what it felt like to have a woman come on to you? Was Sasha...here...now? With him? He stepped closer to her. Her scent filled his senses, the spice of her perfume, the heat of her body. Her hands trembled as they reached over to him and began tracing their way up his arms.

"You don't have a laptop," he pointed out.

"What?"

"You said you needed me to take a look at your laptop," he explained. "But you don't have one with you."

"Oh." Her mouth made a perfectly round circle with that simple word, the tip of her tongue resting on her teeth as her hands cupped his neck, and she pulled herself in close and tight to him. "I must have forgotten it at the office."

Then she pushed up on her tiptoes, and put her trembling lips to his. Tom's body instantly responded and he knew what paradise must feel like. This was everything he had wanted from Sasha but had always been too afraid to take.

No. Not everything.

He wrapped his arms around her petite waist and sealed her body to his. She gasped against his lips as his throbbing erection pressed into her, begging to be let out. The kiss turned hot, and needful, and when she bit his lip he moaned and began walking her backward to the bedroom. This was happening. Right now, this was going to happen.

Her hands found his, and forcefully she pulled them to the front of her. "Here," she instructed him. "Touch me here. I have another lap you can play with."

She pressed his fingers in between her legs, bunching up the fabric of her dress, directing him to her secret notch. She fell against him when he found it through her clothing and her trembling became a forceful spasm that sent her over her edge as she bit down on his shoulder to keep from screaming.

"Tom..." she said, begging him, pleading with him, telling him that she was his to do whatever he wanted to.

In the bedroom, he laid her down on the bed, gently, and helped her pull her dress up to her hips. She took it up further, up over her arms and then her head. She tossed it aside, panting and gasping, prostrate before him.

She wasn't wearing a bra, and the perfect roundness of her breasts struck him as the most beautiful thing he had ever seen. Her white panties were wet, and she took his hands again, and showed him where to touch her.

When he joined her on the bed, she screamed his name. She wanted all he could give her and when he thought she was done, she took him again.

It was hours later when they were naked and sweating and panting in the bed, worn out and still wanting each other. Sasha cried, and wiped away the tears with her fingers, explaining she always cried when a man did her right because nobody knew how to treat a woman anymore. Moments later, she fell asleep from sheer exhaustion.

This wasn't love, he told himself. This was crazy, was what it was. Crazy, and exciting. Now he knew a little more of what made Sasha tick. She wanted to be loved. She wanted tender sex from a man who respected her. He could so be that guy. At least for today.

Then he fell asleep beside her with a smile on his face.

The sky outside was dark when he woke up again. It was the feel of feathery light somethings brushing over his face that had brought him out of a deep, deep sleep. At first, he thought that maybe Sasha was ready to go again. He was sore, to be sure, but he was definitely willing to show her how good a man could be to her again...

Only, in the backsplash from the hallway light he could see that it wasn't Sasha. It was Aubrey.

She wore her hair back in a ponytail now, and she had on a black t-shirt and black pants and black, fingerless leather gloves. He hardly recognized her. This was the bad girl side of her, he realized, the side that he had always known was there but could never hope to enjoy himself.

Looked like his luck had changed with Aubrey, too.

"Wait," he said, whispering so he wouldn't wake up Sasha sleeping next to him. "How did you get in here?"

She winked at him, leaning in close to whisper in his ear. "A girl needs her secrets."

Then she bit his ear. Not gently.

He didn't even have time to cry out. She was standing up over him again already, and he was very aware of how naked he was when she took her time looking him up and down. This was different than the way Sasha had looked at him. There was a hunger in Audrey's gaze. A need to take, and not give. A need to have him in any way she could.

She looked over at Sasha, and sneered. "You've been with the little girl." Grabbing his hand, she pulled him out of bed. "Now come be with a woman."

He stumbled along with her, to the living room, to the couch, like he didn't have a choice. When they got there she pushed him and he stumbled onto the cushions of the sectional, on his hands and knees. She was on him in an instant, reaching around between his legs and grabbing hold of his junk. She squeezed, and he froze.

"Do everything I say," she told him, running her other hand up his side, under his chest, until her fingers found his nipple. "I can make this feel good."

She circled his nipple, and she kneaded his balls, and damn it all to hell if he didn't think his brain was going to explode from the sheer pleasure of it.

Then she yanked on him and he gagged, even as his cock went to full attention in a split second.

"If you don't do what I say," she told him, "I'll make it hurt. We clear?"

She was everything he knew she would be. Forceful, inventive, wild and crazy. He wanted more of this. He wanted her to abuse him. This was the best night of his life! Two girls with wildly different sexual needs, and both of them taking it from him!

This time she used her nails. "I said, are we clear?"

"Yes," he told her.

Somehow she managed to slide under him, through his legs. She was using his hips for leverage. "Good. Now...stay very still."

Her mouth slid over his tip, and his whole body shook from the pleasure of what she did next.

Chapter Three

Tom ached all over when his eyes opened again. In a good way. In a way that he was going to remember for the rest of his life.

He was in bed again, with two beautiful and naked women tangled up with him. Sasha's hand was stroking him gently in his abused crotch, circling the globes of his testicles and drawing designs on the back of his little head with a fingernail. Audrey's mouth was suckling at his nipple. Even in sleep, these two couldn't get enough of him.

Finally arrived, he thought. I'm a stud.

Nestling down in the press of warm bodies, he let himself start to be aroused again. A man never knows his limitations until he comes right up against them. That made him chuckle. "Pun intended," he whispered to himself.

"Shut up," Audrey's sleepy voice ordered him. "Talk when I tell ya to."

"You shut up," Sasha told her. "He's mine, and he can do whatever he wants."

Audrey raised her head, her eyes flashing a warning at the other woman. "He's mine, and he will be obedient or I'll whip him again."

An involuntary twinge clenched Tom's butt cheeks. The whipping had been unexpected, especially with his own belt, but...it had been oddly enjoyable.

As the two of them continued to snarl at each other—over him, he realized with a smile—Tom rolled to the side to check the clock. Damn it!

"Hey, we're all late for work," he told them. "We have to go. Last night was...wow. Last night was beyond amazing. Can we do it again tonight?"

Audrey's hand pushed down on his chest. "You aren't leaving."

"Don't go," Sasha pleaded with him.

"Hey, come on," he chuckled, extricating himself from them with a little effort. "We've got to work. Remember? Paychecks and lives and bills and stuff? We'll do it again. Tonight."

He kissed them both on their foreheads, and went to take a shower. He really needed a shower. And maybe a bandaid for that one spot where Audrey had scratched him.

At the door to the bedroom, he looked back. Both women were sitting there, naked and glorious...and staring at him. Kind of creepy, but hey. Who was he to complain? He'd been screwed by two women last night. And then by the same two women at the same time. The miracle was that they had gotten any sleep last night at all.

He stepped around the corner, and then looked back into the room. They were in the same spot. Staring.

Okay, very creepy, but still.

Nagging thoughts began to pester him while he got cleaned up. Were those two really interested in him? The two of them, falling for his simple geek charms on the same day, just like that? What were the odds? Actually he could pretty much factor the odds in his big brain and they weren't very good. If they weren't into him, though, then why would they be all over him like that...

No. It couldn't be the fortune teller. That old woman with her mumbo jumbo and her pipe and her weird mumbling. There was no such thing as gypsy magic. No way that a spell would make two very different women want to crawl into his bed...and couch...and on the floor...the kitchen table...um.

No way could that be explained by magic. Ridiculous. Sasha and Audrey must be into him for who he was. It was the only thing that made sense to him.

They were gone when he got out of the shower, dressed and ready to go, and he figured that they were going to get ready at their own apartments. After all, showing up to work in the same clothes was a big taboo, right? Especially for women. Not that he didn't want to shout to the world about what he'd gotten last night, but he didn't exactly want it to be spread around the office, either. No sense getting anyone in trouble at the vaunted offices of Jansen and Howe.

So, he smiled, and locked the door behind him, and whistled his way to work.

He did his work in his cubicle all day, fixing coding problems and resetting passwords and whatever else the company needed from him for the day. All the while, his thoughts were on last night, and on what might happen tonight. There were a few things left on his list of sexual fetishes that he wanted to try yet. One woman who was incredibly submissive, and one who was a closet dominatrix. Well. That did lead to a lot of possibilities.

He was hard all day long, just thinking about it.

Around lunchtime he snuck his way up to the second floor. He figured he would drop in on Audrey, and then Sasha, and confirm their date for tonight on the sly. Only, when he got there, Audrey's front desk was empty. When he asked someone passing by, the guy just shrugged and said she never showed up for work today. No note. No message. Weird he said, because one of the junior associates did the same thing. Sasha something.

Tom stood there long after the guy was gone, trying to figure out what was going on. Both women didn't come into the office. Were they embarrassed by what they had done? Did him leaving them there at his apartment this morning make them realize they had made some sort of mistake?

Hot lead twisted into his guts. It couldn't be over between them just like that, could it? One wild night together and then they just ignore him again.

No. No way. He was not going to let that happen. They were into him. He refused to believe it could be anything else. They were just sleeping it off. Sure. It had nothing to do with a spell cast by a con woman selling love potions out of her hole-in-the-wall shop. Making a bee line back to the elevators he took out his cellphone and pulled up both Sasha's and Audrey's numbers from his contacts list. Being in IT had its advantages. He had people's e-mail addresses and cell numbers and a lot of other information he probably shouldn't.

In this case, he had the phone numbers of the two hottest women he knew.

Writing a single text to both of them, he sent it off. *Meet me at my apartment. Now. Need you both.*

After a moment's thought he erased the "both" at the end and just left it as *need you.* That made it more personal.

Then he called his boss and said he still wasn't recovered from whatever he'd caught yesterday. So. He needed another day. After that he went straight home. This was going to be settled today. It was him the girls wanted. They weren't being forced to sleep with him by a spell or anything else. This was what they wanted.

It was what he wanted, too.

Outside his apartment, he hesitated. Was that a sound he'd heard inside? He put his ear to the door, and then shrugged it off. No way. He locked up this morning. No one else had the key. Just him.

Unlocking the door, he went inside and tossed his stuff on the table and pulled out his cellphone again to check for an answering text. Nothing, from either girl. This was crazy. Where were they? He did have their addresses—thank you IT gods—and he could just drop by at either of their places if he wanted. Maybe he should. Was that being a stalker? No, he was just worried about them. That's what it was. Yes. That's what he would do. The girls needed him, after all.

Pain blossomed at the back of his head and he only had enough time to realize he'd been hit with something very hard before the floor rushed up to meet him and the world went dark.

Chapter Four

He came to, still in his own apartment, sitting in a kitchen chair.

In the middle of the living room.

Tied by his hands and feet to the chair.

Naked.

Audrey was kneeling in front of him, as naked as he was, slowly sucking her way up the inside of his leg. When she felt him stirring, she bit the inside of his thigh.

"Ow, hey that hurts. Um...ow...ow!"

She bit down harder, bracing her hands on his legs for leverage, and he saw her eyes roll up into her head as she clamped down hard enough to draw blood.

Tom screamed. He couldn't help it. Waking up like this, to this gorgeous woman...chewing on him...what was going on?

"Shh," he heard Sasha saying to him as her hands smoothed around his neck from behind, and then down his chest. Her cheek nuzzled his, and her tongue licked his face. "Shh. Just trust us. Just let it happen. We want you, Tom. We want you. Let us have you."

Audrey's hand cupped his balls, and squeezed. Tom's scream turned into a squeak.

Sasha licked his lips, and then her teeth nipped at his chin and he was suddenly blubbering, begging her not to bite him there. "Not the face please not the face please don't…"

He felt Audrey's finger jab up between his testicles, and he froze as much as he could with her mouth still sucking at his blood and Sasha's teeth starting to graze the slope of his neck where his jugular was and the stabbing, choking pain in his crotch.

His penis stood tall and erect through it all, somehow turned on while he feared for his life.

Audrey shifted positions between his legs. She knelt there, looking up at him, his blood on her face. "Sasha told you to shush," she ordered him. "If you're a good boy, we'll make this feel good. If you're a bad boy, well…"

Her lips slid over the tip of his cock, down deep, and then deeper, and as she cupped his testicles in both hands she slid up his length again, scraping her teeth along the thin skin the whole way.

He was whimpering now, because he knew what would happen if she chose to bite him now, bite him there, and he nearly fainted when she got right to his tip and sucked him there and squeezed him between her teeth.

Then she was off of him, and he could breathe again.

Sasha whispered in his ear. "We want you."

"F-fine," he stuttered. "Untie m-me and we c-can do what w-we did last n-night. I'd like that. W-wouldn't you l-like that?"

Audrey slapped him, right across his manhood, sending painful vibrations through his gut. "I want him first."

Sasha snorted. "if you have him first there'll be nothing left of him. "Let me have him first."

Tom couldn't believe this. Women fighting over him should be a dream come true. This was a nightmare. "Please," he started to beg.

Audrey slapped him again. "You shut up, unless I tell you that you can speak. Fine, Sasha. You want him first, you take him. Just leave me something."

She stood up and stepped away from him and Tom nearly threw up in relief. If Audrey was going to be that rough with her sex then maybe she wasn't the woman for him. He could just let Sasha do him and then claim he was too tired for Audrey. Yeah. Sure.

He watched as Sasha came around him, naked and dark and steamy with desire. She straddled him and then braced herself with his shoulders to lower herself onto him, inch by inch, until he was in her and she was arching her back and then throwing her head forward into his neck and moaning softly. There, he thought. Yeah, that's better. Even being tied up like this was okay as long as she...as she...

Her lips suckled at his ear, and then her teeth tore into his flesh.

He screamed as she rocked herself on him, tearing off his earlobe and sexing herself to an intense tremor that curled her toes and wracked her whole body.

Tom felt the pain. He felt the blood pouring down his neck. She took a bite of him! Oh, damn oh damn oh damn damn damn she bit off part of his ear! They didn't just want him...they wanted to eat him! They were going to eat him!

When she got off him, spitting out blood and wiping her mouth with her arm, she leaned in close again. He cringed, terrified that she was going to take another bite out of him. Instead she smiled, and whispered into his ruined ear. "Thank you for that."

Sasha pushed Audrey aside. "My turn."

"What do you want from me?" he screamed, his voice unnervingly high and cracking with tight emotions that ranged from horror to disgust to abject fear. "What do you want!"

The two women froze. They stared at him. Audrey was caught in the motion of reaching for him, for his softening male member and his bloody leg. They stood there still as statues, their eyes riveted to him.

"What do you want?" he said through sudden tears. This couldn't be happening. This was insane! "What do you want?"

A new voice caught his attention. A raspy voice accented by Italian heritage. "They want what I want, Tom. Don't worry. Let me explain. Ladies, please move."

Sasha and Audrey both stepped aside obediently, their eyes still on them, their scent still carrying a desire for sex. Behind them, Madame Toufou stepped forward, leaning on her cane. Her clothes were just as colorful today as they had been yesterday. At least she wasn't smoking on her pipe, Tom thought crazily. The landlord would never give him the damage deposit back if she got ashes in the carpet.

He was losing his grip, he realized. He was bleeding from his leg and his ear—she bit his ear!—and he was too scared to think straight. "You," he managed to say. "What are you doing here?"

Madame Toufou cackled. "When you were in my shop I saw that you have personal wealth. I desire that, Tom. That is what we want from you."

"You...you're robbing me?"

"Oh, don't be so crass," she barked. "I gave you a night you will never forget for as long as you live, correct? That was what you wanted. A night with these two. I have delivered. Now, I want something for myself."

"But I paid you!"

"You did, yes, but I know you have more. I want it, Tom. You hide a large part of your money from the IRS. I saw that in my reading of your aura. That means it is in this apartment. Tell me where you hide the money, Tom, and I will leave."

"What about them?" he blurted, his voice still strained. "Why are they doing this?"

Madame Toufou frowned like he was annoying her. "Ladies, please kiss each other."

Sasha and Audrey stepped off to the side, together, and obediently pressed their blood-stained lips together, moaning with pleasure as they squirmed against each other's nakedness and kissed with passion.

"There," the old gypsy woman said to Tom. "Do you understand now?"

Tom's jaw dropped open. The pain became a distant concern as the reality of his situation hit him. This was why the two women had suddenly become interested in him. It was a spell. Madame Toufou was controlling Sasha and Audrey. It was impossible.

Yet it was real.

She snapped her fingers in front of his face to get his attention back. "Tell me where the money is. Now."

"You'll let them go?"

Madame Toufou blinked at him. Then she threw her head back and cackled so hard she choked on phlegm and began hacking in his face. "You're worried about them? You should be worried about yourself!"

"I'll tell you where the money is if you promise to let them go." He didn't know where this newfound bravery was from but he felt it fierce in his chest. He needed them to be safe. Even if their night together hadn't meant anything to them because they were being forced into it, the night had meant everything to him and he needed to know they would be safe.

He glanced at them as they continued to kiss and fondle each other. He had to look away. How did this happen? How could it happen? Was it hypnosis, or a hallucinogenic drug or something?

"Fine," the old hag snapped at him. "I promise they will be free of me when you give me your money. There. That good enough for you?"

It was going to have to be. "Under the couch," he mumbled. "There's a hidden compartment under the couch."

She nodded, and shuffled off. From where he was tied he couldn't see what she was doing, but he heard the couch being heaved aside and then the sound of the floorboards being pried up, and then her delighted gasp as she found his lockbox with the twenty thousand dollars in it.

"Good, good!" She cackled some more, and then toddled back into view, leaning on the cane and holding the rectangular metal box in the crook of her other arm. "That concludes our business, I believe."

She turned to leave. Three steps later, she thumped her cane on the floor hard enough that a *boom* swept across the room.

"Finish this," she said without looking back.

In the next moment there were two voracious women all over him, desiring him, needing him, taking him...

Devouring him.

Through the blood and the pain and the intense sexual arousal Tom saw Madame Toufou close the apartment door behind her.

Audrey hit him. Sasha bit into his chest. Their fingernails clawed into his flesh. Their breasts were in his face. Their hands touched him everywhere as parts of him were torn away, as his fingers were broken, as they took him apart...piece...by...piece...

Epilogue

The police arrived a day later at the request of the landlord. A foul odor had been reported from inside the apartment. Death had a smell all its own, the officers would later explain.

Inside, they found the gruesome remains of a man tied to a chair. There wasn't much left to identify. His head had rolled away across the floor.

At his feet, two naked women lay in each other's embrace, chunks torn out of their bodies by teeth and hands and methods the officers could only guess at. Their lips were still pressed together.

Pieces of the man, later identified as Tom Henderson a virtually unknown IT geek, were found in the women's fingers...and teeth...

FRANKIE

STEVE RINKLES

Frankie closed the trailer door and winced when it gave a loud click as it shut. She stood in the cold air in her denim shorts and her brother's old Van Halen t-shirt and listened. She could hear only the birds slowly waking up in the pale blue morning light. She half-expected to hear the familiar thunder of her daddy's voice to come through, demanding breakfast and coffee, but he hadn't seen eight in the morning since he lost his job five years ago, so she felt safe enough. She touched the five dollars in her pocket to make sure it was still there, then she headed towards the woods.

Happy Heavens was enormous as trailer parks went around here, but Frankie had it all mapped out it her head with the quietest routes to anywhere she'd want to go at any time of day or night. It helped that their two-tone rust bucket of a trailer was in the far back, near the woods, with no neighbors. If she needed to go to the store right now, she knew who would still be asleep and who would leave her alone if they happened to see her passing. She knew exactly how to avoid any assholes and do-gooders. It was a five-minute run; speed was important when daddy was out of beer. If she had a half-hour free from chores and had finished her latest library book then she could get to the playground in the suburb nearby in ten minutes without having to see anyone who knew her. They had fewer swings and only a pretty pathetic baby's slide there, but Happy Heavens' playground was where all the dealers hung out, so that was a no-go zone. Her daddy told her she was too old for swings at fourteen. She thought maybe that's why she still liked them, because he didn't.

Today, Frankie was headed to the east side of town, so she had to walk through the woods at the edge of the trailer park for a while to avoid a couple of the biggest assholes, then cut through for the last third of the park and come out onto the road safe and sound and unseen.

The circus was in town, and Frankie had never seen a circus.

Nothing much came to Waleska, Georgia, so she couldn't pass this up. She smiled to herself. She knew it would probably be closed, but she wanted to just see it, maybe even walk around a little.

If there are elephants there, she thought, I'm gonna flip out!

Frankie hopped the fence and landed with a crunch on the fallen leaves that covered the ground. She walked ten feet into the trees to be sure no-one could see her and to enjoy the sound of the birds. She lived with her headphones on, listening over and over to her brother's old punk rock mix tapes, but she enjoyed the sound of the real world when hardly anyone was awake in it.

A cracking sound ahead caught her attention, but she was too late to avoid being spotted.

"Motherfucker," a voice came, "I thought we talked about this?"

It was Heinrich. He was nearly twenty, balding before his time and only few cheeseburgers shy of a heart attack. He was dressed in army clothes and he gave a toothy grin. When Frankie saw his air rifle she froze.

"These aren't your woods," he said, looking confused, "are they?"

Frankie started walking backwards.

"In fact," he said, "I remember a chat we had where we discussed this, like, at length."

If Heinrich was here... she thought.

An arm grabbed her from behind and locked around her head tight.

"Get off me, you son of a bitch!" she shouted.

Heinrich was in hysterics, laughing his ass off. Frankie pushed her way free of the headlock and jumped back. It was Henry, Heinrich's younger brother. He was about half his brother's size, lengthwise and width wise, with a half-grown mustache and a lisp.

"Did you say something about mom?" Henry said, lisping his way through the S's.

Frankie ran back towards her trailer. She knew she could outrun both of them. "Fuck your mom!" she shouted, immediately disappointing herself, but they deserve it, she thought.

She could hear them stampeding through the leaves after her. When she was twenty yards ahead she turned sharply and tried to loop back past them. As she did, she felt a sharp sting in the side of her knee that buckled it and sent her tumbling to the ground. She screamed and looked up as Henry and Heinrich walked over.

"Shit," Heinrich said, laughing and holding up his air rifle, "I'm pretty good with this thing!"

Henry didn't laugh. Henry rarely laughed. He had the same half-scowl for all occasions.

"What the fuck did you say about our mom?" Henry said.

He kicked Frankie in the side, causing her to curl up like one of those bugs that she used to play with when she was a little girl; she was a human roly poly. Henry stood on her back and then sat down on top of her, pressing the air out of her lungs. He grabbed both of her arms and twisted them back as she cried out.

"Apologize!" Henry said.

"I'm sorry!" Frankie said.

Heinrich stood over her and pointed the air rifle at her head.

"Don't!" Frankie said. "Please!"

Heinrich laughed. "Hold her still," he said. He put his air rifle on his back and picked up a handful of dry leaves off the ground. He bent down as far as his belly would allow with the leaves in his hand and said, "Open up, bitch."

Frankie squirmed and tried to shake herself free in a blind panic. She hated dirt. She couldn't stand bugs. She wanted to die right there and then. More than anything in the world, she wanted to die immediately so she wouldn't have to do this. It wasn't normal to be this afraid of bugs and dirt, she knew that. She couldn't explain it. But she couldn't control it either. There was no reasoning with the fear. It overwhelmed her.

Heinrich shoved the leaves against her mouth, but she wouldn't open up.

"You scared?" Heinrich said. "Ha! She's scared of bugs, I guess! What a geek!"

Henry twisted her arms back more and when she screamed Heinrich shoved the leaves in.

Then, Henry laughed.

"Eat up, little squirrel!" Heinrich said, almost crying with laughter.

The leaves tasted foul and scratched the roof of Frankie's mouth. She convulsed violently to get free and spat them out, screaming and thrashing, and Henry got off, having had his fun and enjoying watching her frantic display.

"If we see you in here again," Henry said, "I'm gonna bring my daddy's gun. And that doesn't shoot pellets, you get me?"

Frankie stood and wiped the tears from her eyes and the dried bits of leaves from her mouth.

"You get me, little squirrel?" he said again.

She nodded, scowling

Heinrich cleared his throat and spat on Frankie's t-shirt. "Van Halen sucks," he said.

Frankie was shaking as she brushed her hair out of her eyes and wiped the dirt from her face. She took slow steps backwards away from them and in the direction of the circus. She turned and started walking, slower than before, limping a little, her face burning with shame.

"Ugly bitch!" Heinrich shouted after her.

He fired his air rifle in her direction again, hitting a nearby tree.

Frankie ran. The harder she ran and the farther away she got from Happy Heavens, the less she cried.

It was always the same.

Whether it was her daddy or any other asshole, Frankie always ended up running.

Frankie felt worthless and pathetic and alone. The anger would come later.

This is how it always was.

*

Waleska, Georgia, wasn't much to look at. There was very little in the way of redeeming features, as far as Frankie could see, other than it being smaller than most places and therefore having fewer people. The population had only in the last decade or so crept up over five thousand, thanks largely to the boom in the popularity of trailer parks after the economy died a death. The owner of Happy Heavens was making a killing, but there were few local businesses and therefore there was no real reason for anyone to be in town. This meant that mornings were quiet. You could walk down the main street and not see a single car. Frankie headed down past the auto repair shop where her daddy used to work, before the bad times. She went around the high school she rarely attended and cut through the football field to avoid seeing the intersection where a truck took away her mom and her older brother. A half-mile in she cut back onto the same road and saw the circus tent rising up over the trees ahead.

Frankie couldn't bring herself to smile again yet after the beating she took, but she was starting to put it to the back of her mind. For the time being, she had scolded herself for being pathetic, cursed herself seven ways from Sunday, and decided that it was OK because one day she would leave this place. She had decided the same thing a hundred times before, of course, but the promise still helped her to cope. She'd developed a knack for dealing with these kinds of beatings over the years. It was almost a skill.

The circus was pitched in a field with a red banner hung from the border fence. "Bakker Bros. World Famous Circus!" it said, showing a grinning clown face and a trapeze artist mid-jump. The big top tent was white with red stripes and as high as a three-story building. Frankie ran up to the gate and she spotted bumper cars, hoop games and popcorn stands. She couldn't see any people.

Frankie climbed over the gate and walked carefully up to the corner of a closed-up hot dog truck nearby. She peered around it. No alarms sounded and no dogs barked, so she decided to take a walk around.

The sky was brightening some now, and, though she wished she could see it at night all lit up, Frankie was captivated by the place. Most of Frankie's time was taken up by chores, but the rest she devoted to reading. She didn't like science fiction or horror or anything too old. She jumped from book to book as fast as she could, and she loved more than anything to read about faraway places – *real* places – and imagine that one day she could visit them. She had read about circuses, seen them on TV when she was allowed to watch, and visiting one had made it onto her mental list of things she'd do once she was free, when she had her own place - a house, not a trailer - and her own money and no-one to tell her what to do. Frankie used to consider running away all the time, crafting elaborate plans and staring at maps, but now her plans had been replaced with a simple deep longing to be somewhere else. She didn't want to get her hopes up with place names and deadlines. Once, she really tried to leave. She took her school backpack, filled it with canned food, stole twenty bucks from her daddy, and bought a bus ticket. She was found three towns over on the same day and beaten so hard she ended up in the infirmary. She was twelve years old. Since then, she didn't make real plans. Instead, she spent her days running away in small ways, through her route maps of the trailer park, through staying in her room and pretending to go to sleep earlier than she really did, and through her books and tapes.

Reality, for Frankie, meant chores and shouting and punches and cruel names and no friends, so she shut out as much of it as she could.

A haunted house caught Frankie's eye with wooden cut-out ghosts and a deep-sea diver that looked just like the one in *Scooby Doo*. She was easily tall enough to get in, but it was shut, the cars covered with plastic sheets. The cars were built for two people, she noticed. She wondered what it would be like to be able to notice something like that without feeling sad.

"You work here?" a voice came.

Frankie raised her eyebrows and looked to see an Indian man staring at her with a look of confusion. He was tall and dark-skinned with long, black hair and he wore jeans and an Atari t-shirt. He looked about thirty years old and his accent was pure California. He had tattoos on his arms, Frankie noticed, but they were just big, black blotches, as if they were once normal tattoos that had now been filled in and covered up. They looked like leopard spots.

Frankie fidgeted with her hands a second and nodded.

"What do you do?" the man asked.

"I - uh..." Frankie started. Behind the Indian man she saw a midget walking past. He looked like the clown on the banner, but he was wearing shorts and t-shirt and carrying a Chihuahua. He looked at Frankie and nodded good morning.

"I'm..." she tried again.

"You can't be here," the Indian man said. "If the boss catches you, he'll lose his shit."

"What do you do here?" Frankie said. "I've never been to a circus."

"You can't be here, kid," he said. "Come on."

The Indian man walked over and put his hand on her back to usher her back towards the gate. When Frankie flinched away from his slight touch, he stopped and his face softened as he looked at her. Frankie didn't know what he was looking at, but she didn't like to be touched. She didn't like people looking at her.

I just want to see the goddamn elephants, she thought, her stomach turning with disappointment.

The combined fear and hurt and hope made Frankie feel sick. And it made her look scared.

"I tell you what," the Indian man said, "what if I could get you some tickets for tonight's show?"

"I can't," she said. "I have things to do. Daddy would be mad."

The Indian man looked like he was becoming impatient or angry, Frankie couldn't tell which. He looked all around to see if anyone was watching, then, seeing no-one, he lightened up.

"Alright," he said, putting on a smile. "How about a tour? I don't think the boss is around, so it should be alright."

Frankie's eyes lit up. "Do you have elephants?"

The Indian man laughed. "We have one, yeah. You want to meet her?"

Frankie nodded, feeling joyful tears hit her eyes at the very thought of it.

"What's your name?" he asked.

"Frankie," she said.

"Francesca?"

Her mom used to call her Francesca.

"I'm sorry," he said. "Frankie, it is. My name's Tommy."

"Tommy?"

"Tommy Hawk," he said with a smile. "Let's go this way."

They started walking past the big top tent.

He whispered, "It's not really, but that's what the posters say. My real name's Teddy."

Frankie smiled. That was a much better name, she thought. "Where are you from?" she asked.

"I'm from LA originally."

"No, I mean... Um..."

"Oh," Teddy laughed. "I'm Cheyenne through and through."

"There was a boy in school was a... uh..."

"You can say Indian," Teddy said. "It's not a dirty word. What tribe was he from?"

"He was a Cheyenne, too," she said.

"Then that's what call him, a Cheyenne. Not many of us left. Here we are."

They'd arrived at a smaller tent. It wasn't designed for visitors and looked more like a military tent. A sign outside said, simply, "Animals".

"Is there really an elephant in there?" Frankie asked. "You're not shitting me?"

Teddy laughed. "No shit, Frankie."

The tent was empty but for two large cages and buckets of some kind of animal feed. The first cage was empty. Teddy looked shocked for a second and whispered, "Oh, God, no! The tiger's escaped!"

"Shut up," Frankie said, grinning. "I'm not an idiot."

"No, you're not," Teddy said with a nod. "Frankie, meet Tabitha."

Tabitha was gray and wrinkled with pock-marked skin and small course hairs on her head. She was the size of a van. Her trunk touched the ground and was curled up slightly. Her tail flicked here and there. She was very still otherwise, only moving her head slightly when she saw her visitors. Frankie ran up to the cage and put her hands on the bars.

"She's beautiful!" Frankie said with a wide grin. "Come here, girl."

The elephant moved back a little. Its eyes, old and tired around the outside but vivid and alive within, watched Frankie warily. Tabitha's enormous ears twitched as a fly buzzed around her head.

"How old is she?" Frankie asked.

"She's ten, I think," Teddy said.

"Is that old?"

"She's still a baby. Elephants can live until they're sixty, you know?"

Frankie was impressed. She smiled and tried again to reach out to touch Tabitha, but Tabitha backed away. Something about her troubled Frankie. In the twitches of her ears, the light flap of her tail and the shifting of her great weight on her feet, Tabitha looked nervous. Frankie noticed her cage was only somewhat bigger than the elephant herself, and food was piled on the ground and left uneaten.

Teddy noticed Frankie's smile starting to fade.

"She's, uh, very friendly usually," Teddy said. "She's scared of new people, I guess."

Frankie drew her hand out. "Does she come out of the cage much?"

"Only for shows," Teddy said, grimacing a little.

Tabitha turned in her cage to face away from them.

"We better leave her rest," Teddy said.

Frankie noticed whip marks on the elephant's back.

Teddy caught her looking at them and started walking away from the cage, expecting Frankie to follow. "Come on," he said. "You want to see where I work?"

Frankie looked at Tabitha a little longer. Tabitha didn't look back.

Maybe she doesn't like to be looked at or touched either, Frankie thought.

*

Teddy worked out of a small, brightly colored gypsy caravan.

"Cheyennes don't live in these, do they?" Frankie said.

"No," Teddy said, "but it's all the same to the whites who run this place. They don't think anyone can tell the difference."

Inside was decorated with clay and wooden ornaments of owls, deer and wolves, and feathers hung on strings from the roof. A compartment at the back, behind a curtain, had just enough room for a small refrigerator, a television set, an old Nintendo and a bunk.

"What do you do?" Frankie asked.

"Tattoos," Teddy said. "Mostly temporary tattoos of Indian designs. Sometimes I have to branch out into face-painting for the kids to make a little more money. I can do real tattoos, though. I taught myself a long time ago. I got pretty good at it."

"Were you in prison?" Frankie played with a feather that was laid on a table in the middle. Teddy sat down.

"I was," Teddy said, going into the back. "I'm not so scary, though."

"I know," Frankie said.

"Here," Teddy said, handing her a soda pop. "You eaten anything today?"

Frankie's face turned red. "Leaves," she said. She sat down and held the feather in her hand. She looked at it so she wouldn't have to look at Teddy. He was a do-gooder, she could see that now. The trailer park was full of them. A hundred times Frankie had walked around with a black eye or cigarette burns on her arms and people would stop her and say how terrible it all was, but none of them would ever do anything for her. They thought saying was enough, but it wasn't.

She didn't want words.

"Your daddy make you do that?" Teddy said.

Frankie shook her head. Teddy handed her a Twinkie and she opened it up, smiling a sad thank you.

"Hey," Teddy said, "how about I give you a tattoo? A little one? I can do a little elephant for you."

"My daddy wouldn't like that."

"Just a temporary one. I can do it at the top of your arm there, where he wouldn't see."

Frankie's hands shook as she nibbled her Twinkie. "He'd see," she said, "wherever it was."

Teddy went into the back and came back with a beer for himself, opening it with his teeth and spitting the bottle cap out on the floor. As he had his back turned, Frankie wolfed down the Twinkie. She didn't like people to see her eat. Teddy sat and drank - he appeared changed in some undefinable way - and Frankie had some of her soda. Frankie saw that Teddy's hand was shaking a little, too.

"Can I tell you a story?" Teddy said.

"Sure, I don't mind," Frankie said.

"A long time ago - I'm talking about the 1800s, now - there was a village of Cheyenne people and some others down in Colorado. They used to have a great big piece of land, until, one day, someone struck gold nearby. Then, the government came on down and they took that land away from my people. Some of my people agreed. They signed contracts they couldn't read, took gifts, and then they found themselves cooped up with nowhere to go, like Tabitha back there. After a while, some of the Cheyenne, they didn't like this, so they started to get angry. They started leaving the cage that had been made for them, riding and hunting in the old lands they used to own."

"Like in movies?" Frankie said.

"Just like in the movies, riding and shooting guns and arrows with their shirts off and all that great stuff. Then there came the war, and lots of soldiers came with it. And to the white men, my people weren't worth a damn. All they could see was land, lots of it, which my people had the nerve to live on. There was a chief at this village, he'd been to the White House, you know? The president himself had given him an American flag. And he was so proud, this chief. He'd raise that flag every day over the village. And when he heard that soldiers had been going around the country, murdering his people? He said, 'No. This will not happen to us. We are Americans.' Even when the soldiers rolled up on his village, he just raised that flag. The men were all out hunting that day, leaving only women, kids and the old folks. And this chief gathered everyone up and said, 'If you stand under this flag, nothing bad will happen to you.' So they did. Have you heard about this in school?"

Frankie shook her head.

"You won't. The white men call it The Battle of Sand Creek. My people had a different name for it: The Sand Creek Massacre. Nearly a thousand soldiers rode in there and murdered a hundred and fifty, two hundred people - women, children, old folks. And they murdered them good, let me tell you. Even the babies. They took trophies so they could show off to their friends back home: ears, noses; they'd even skin the tattoo off someone as a keepsake."

Frankie was starting to feel a little sick.

Teddy nodded. "Yep," he said. "My daddy used to tell me all about this stuff. 'That's how the white man's world works,' he'd say. Because, you see, Frankie, white men take and take and take and they convince you that it's for the best. They take everything you have, and they get you so scared and so beaten down that eventually you have to convince yourself that you're happy with what you got, because otherwise what's the point in living?"

Frankie put the feather down on the table. Teddy swigged his beer and took a deep breath, trying not to look angry, but Frankie could still see it.

"Let me give you a tattoo," Teddy said, putting down his bottle. "A real one."

Frankie swallowed. She didn't want to say no to him when he looked that upset.

"I have some special ink," he said. He leaned in and lowered his voice. "People like those who you met today, people like your daddy, they don't give you respect. They don't treat you like a human being, right? Growing up Cheyenne, I know all about that. It nearly took my life, but then I got myself an education, a dark education, you get me?"

Frankie was quiet. She hugged her arm with her hand and her leg was shaking.

"You can't be afraid your whole life, Frankie," Teddy said. "Let me help you. No-one will ever touch you again, I promise you that."

Frankie wanted to say yes.

"There are forces in this world that men like that haven't even *dreamed* of."

Frankie wanted to say yes. Teddy walked into his bedroom compartment and pulled up the carpet in the corner. Underneath, in a small, dark gap, was a wooden box with horses carved into it. Teddy brought it back and laid it on the table.

"This isn't Cheyenne stuff I'm talking about here. This isn't some kind of Indian magic bullshit," he said. "This is the real deal. The ink that's in this box will give you all the help you'll ever need. You won't have to ask for it, it'll just come. This ink will connect you with the earth itself. This is dark shit. This is low magic. The dark and the low creatures, they'll become your friends. You'll never have to be afraid of anyone. You'll never had to run from anything ever again."

Frankie wanted to say yes. "Are you tricking me?" she said.

Teddy took her hand and looked her in the eye. She tried to pull her hand back at first but then she looked up at him. She could see in his eyes a lifetime's worth of anger, but also compassion. "I don't want your money, Frankie. People like you and me," he said, "we have to look out for one another."

"OK," Frankie said. "Do it."

Teddy nodded. He opened the box. Inside was an ink bottle, a series of different sized needles and a small wooden stick.

"The design is very specific," Teddy said.

"It's not an elephant, is it?" Frankie said.

"No. Roll up your sleeve."

"What is it?"

Frankie turned up the sleeve of her baggy t-shirt. Underneath was a large, sore bruise. Teddy clenched his fist when he saw it. He looked at her and said, "It's a snake."

*

Frankie's tattoo burned her skin as she jumped over the fence and got back on the road home. She had tears in her eyes and a little blood was seeping out from under the bandage. Walking back in the full light of day, Frankie felt like she had emerged from a dream in which she'd made a horrible mistake. She took the long path back through the trailer park which stayed well clear of Henry and Heinrich's trailer and out of the woods. When she got home it was ten o' clock and she knew her daddy would be waking up soon. The trailer, once painted green and white but now mostly green with mold and brown with weathering, was little bigger than Tabitha's cage.

The door closed behind her and she stopped and held her breath for a moment, listening for signs that her daddy was awake. There was nothing. Frankie went into the tiny bathroom, no bigger than an airplane bathroom, she imagined, and she rolled up her sleeve. Unpeeling the bandage from the bottom, Frankie got her first look at the design. The ink was a deep black and spots of blood surrounded it. The long, thick snake was wrapped around the top of her arm, its head resting just under her shoulder. The snake's scales were intricate patterns that looked like words in a long-forgotten language. It didn't look like any Indian drawing she'd ever seen. The snake was angular and almost mathematical-looking.

"Cool," she whispered, but she couldn't shake the sickness in her stomach, the knowledge of what her daddy would do if he saw it.

Wiping away the blood, Frankie pulled on a long-sleeve t-shirt and began tidying up the trailer ready for her daddy. When a low moan sounded from the bedroom, Frankie went in to begin their daily routine. Her daddy's legs weren't what they were before the crash. It was a long time since he wrapped the car around a tree and killed his wife and son. Somehow, the physical pain remained. It would come and go. Sometimes it was a dull ache that caused him to be irritable, other times it was a sharp agony which meant he couldn't walk more than a few steps, sending him to the bottle, to shouting, to violence.

Opening her daddy's bedroom door, Frankie saw him sat on the edge of his bed with his head in his hands.

Today is a bad day, she thought.

"What are you lookin' at?" he said, without turning his head. "I can hear you sneaking around from a mile away."

'Want some breakfast?" Frankie said.

Her daddy grunted. Frankie went to prepare bacon and eggs. He followed her through, leaning on the walls and on the kitchen units, groaning in pain. A small patch of wetness on Frankie's arm started to nag at her attention.

It's still bleeding, she thought.

She tried to turn herself away from her daddy at every opportunity as he shuffled by and slumped onto the sofa chair beside the dining table. His face was drawn and gray beneath permanent stubble and the dark eyes and red nose of a habitual drunk. As Frankie lay his breakfast on the table in front of him, his half-glazed eyes fell on her shoulder. On seeing his daughter bleeding, his first words were, "I didn't do that."

Frankie said nothing. She took out a single Pop Tart for herself and jumped up and sat on the counter to nibble at it.

"What you do?" her daddy said.

"I just cut myself on a branch in the woods," she said, trying to sound relaxed as every muscle in her body tensed. "It's nothin.'"

Through a mouthful of bacon, her daddy said, "I decide what's nothin'. Come here."

"It's OK," she said, forcing a smile. "I'm OK."

"I ain't askin' if you're OK," he said. "I'm asking what you done to your goddamn arm."

Frankie sat and took a small bite of her breakfast. She was shutting down. Her eyes fixed on a spot on the wall opposite. Her legs stopped swinging. She didn't even swallow her breakfast, rather, she chewed it gently as if stuck in a loop. She let herself enter the loop automatically. Trouble would either begin or go away and all she could do was wait and see.

"Come over here, right now," her daddy said.

Trouble had begun.

"What the hell have you been doing around here?" he said. He stood.

"It's nothin;" Frankie said, the loop dissolving under the pressure. "I got beat up," she said quickly.

Her daddy scowled at her. "Who?" he said.

"It doesn't-"

"If you tell me one more time what does or doesn't matter in my own house then you can get out and never come back."

"It was Henry and Heinrich," she said. "Those guys are assholes."

"Did you hit them first?" he said.

"No! I told you, they're assholes. They always hit me!"

"You musta done something," her daddy said, pointing. "I know their mom pretty good. She's a good friend of mine. You better go over there right now and apologize."

Frankie felt as if she'd been hit in the stomach, again.

"Apologize for what?"

"You better get your skinny ass over there right now and tell them you're sorry for whatever you did or I'm gonna make you sorry."

Her daddy came around the table and stood right in front of her. He snatched her Pop Tart from her and threw it to the floor. Frankie looked at her shoes.

"You hearing me, girl?" her daddy said. "I have had just about enough of your shit."

"I didn't do anything," she mumbled.

"What?"

"I didn't do *nothing*," she said.

"Lift up your face," her daddy said. "Lift it up. Look at me."

Frankie slowly lifted her head to look at her daddy. As she got high enough to look up into his eyes, his open hand slapped across Frankie's face with a clack. She turned and put her face in her hands. Through her own sobs she could hear him.

"I say what you've done around here," her daddy said. "I'm not having the whole park thinking I'm keeping a troublemaker."

He grabbed her arm and yanked her down to the floor. She hit hard and didn't want to get back up. From her position on the floor she could see underneath the sofa, into the trailer's hidden places. Something was moving in the dark, she thought. Looking closer, ignoring her daddy's insults, she could see that the darkness was alive.

Everything was moving in there.

The darkness had a hundred legs and a hundred eyes. Her daddy pulled her to her feet and grabbed a walking crutch and threw her out the trailer door.

"We're going visiting, you little shit," he said.

*

Henry and Heinrich's trailer was twice as long as Frankie's and built into a ramshackle L-shape with an extension crafted from scrap wood and plastic sheets which acted as a tool shed and (not very) secret meth lab. Her daddy stumbled as best he could through the mud behind Frankie, hurling curses at her the whole way. Frankie had stopped proclaiming her innocence. She had resigned herself to humiliation.

But something inside her was ready.

Frankie felt a kind of stillness. She had felt acceptance before. She had taken the beatings and everything else and put it to the back of her mind. This wasn't the same. This acceptance felt different. Her face burned red, but not with shame. For the first time, she was angry on schedule, as needed, and she felt something of a purpose rising within her.

The darkness in the trailer had given her a glimmer of how the world really is - a disgusting, ferocious hole into which the human race had fallen - and it had given her a glimpse of what she could be in this world. The darkness was coming to her, she was convinced of that.

As she thought about it, her pace quickened to the point where her daddy had to slow her down. She could feel the darkness following her. The long grass moved in her wake. The leaves rustled. Tiny legs silently followed. Tiny eyes watched. Frankie felt them. She could feel the darkness at her back and it gave her strength. Her calmness now was not the silence of defeat. It was the calm before the storm.

"Henry!" her daddy shouted in an amused tone as they approached. "Heinrich! Get out here, you sorry sons of bitches."

Frankie stopped when she saw them emerge from their trailer, looking half-confused and full-drunk. Henry was in a bathrobe. Heinrich wore only dirty underpants, but he was carrying a shotgun.

"What you want, old man?" Henry shouted.

Frankie stood frozen to the spot, but her daddy hit her with his walking crutch and pointed her towards to the trailer. Frankie could feel a pressure building in her head. She could hear a low ringing noise which was becoming more and more intolerable. The darkness was with her and she was fighting the urge to go back to her room to read her books, to pretend her life was bearable, to pretend her daddy still loved her deep down and that the world had something it was going to offer her one day, that she had a future. Every time her daddy hit her and poked her with the crutch, it chipped away at that idea of a future. It made it harder for Frankie to refuse the darkness.

"Your mom home, boys?" Frankie's daddy said. "Me and Frankie here need to talk with her. With you, too."

The brothers looked at one another with sly smiles.

"Come on in," Henry said.

Frankie had been taken to other trailers before. The men who lived in them, Frankie's routes through the park took her nowhere near them. She could see where this night was headed and she was almost relieved. What they were doing, for Frankie, made her thoughts OK. What they had planned, it justified the onset of the darkness that nipped at her heels. She felt like she could give herself to the dark and low creatures of the world completely. She would let them take what they wanted of these men, so that no man would ever take anything of her again.

She didn't know what the darkness had in store, but it felt big, final.

The interior of the trailer looked like an indoor junkyard and smelled like a cow shed. Oily car parts covered the table, beer cans covered the floor, decade-old pornographic magazine pin-ups decorated the walls and a skinned and treated deer hung headless over the kitchen sink. Frankie stepped inside and Heinrich was directly behind her. She could feel his breath on the back of her neck as he giggled.

Behind the giggling and the small talk and the blaring television which called the plays on a college football game, Frankie could hear a whispering and a sneaking and a crawling. A dark cloud was descending upon the trailer as these men laughed and joked and scratched their crotches and spat on their own floor. Their mother was in the master bedroom. Frankie was led in by her daddy. The woman was sick and lying under a thin, dirty green sheet tucked under her chin, like a gray turtle stuck on its back and doomed to die. At first glance, Frankie thought she was dead, but then she tried to speak. It was German. It was mumbled. It barely qualified as words.

"Looking good, Eva," Frankie's daddy said, standing beside Frankie, cornering her next to the living corpse, the dying turtle. Henry stood at the foot of the bed, watching with his beady eyes. Heinrich's huge frame blocked the doorway. "I hate to bother you," Frankie's daddy said, "but I understand there's been some trouble."

Eva said something else that wasn't words, her ashen face barely moving.

Frankie's daddy looked at Henry.

"She says Frankie is a bitch," Henry said without a hint of a smile. Heinrich chuckled.

"I'm real sorry," Frankie's daddy said. "Truly, I am. I don't know what to do with the girl."

Eva stared at the ceiling, passive, distant. She coughed and speckles of phlegm jumped out of her mouth and onto her face.

"Momma says something should be done," Henry said.

Frankie's fist balled up. She stared a hole through the wall almost, looking straight ahead. Her jaws locked together and the pressure was so hard she thought her teeth might bend and break. Her eyes were stinging with tears. She didn't want anything to happen, but she could feel the pressure building in her head. One of two bad things was about to happen, she knew. It would either be the old bad thing - the thing that had haunted her sleep, which she had spent her waking hours trying to escape from both physically and mentally - or it would be some kind of new bad thing.

"How much money you boys got between you?" Frankie's daddy asked.

They looked Frankie over. Henry said, "We got enough."

Teddy's words returned to Frankie in a loop: "They take and take and take and take and take." His words echoed in her head. "They take everything you have, and they get you so scared and so beaten down that eventually you have to convince yourself that you're happy with what you got, because otherwise what's the point in living?"

Her daddy grabbed her arm and shoved her out past Henry and Heinrich and into the other bedroom. The two brothers were laughing. Tears ran down Frankie's face, but she slowed down her actions, made herself aware of her surroundings. There was one dirty window, broken in one corner and too grimy to let much light through. Stacks of detective and pornographic magazines filled much of the room. Cobwebs dangled from the corners.

"You don't mind if I pull up a chair?" Frankie's daddy said.

Teddy's words returned to Frankie: "That's how the white man's world works."

"Lie on the bed," Henry said.

Frankie sat on the edge of the bed. Her tattoo was a burning pain and a constant reminder of the power she had been promised by Teddy, a power that she could feel growing as the world grew dimmer.

"What the hell is that?" Heinrich said. "The little squirrel got a tattoo?"

He lifted up her sleeve and tore off the bandage. Frankie looked at it. The snake design looked to her to be perfect. It was like looking at the blueprints of a well-designed building, she thought. It had stopped bleeding. It didn't even look sore any more. It had healed.

It looked as though it had always been there.

"What?!" her daddy stood up and grabbed her arm from the other side of the bed and yanked her over to him, almost pulling her arm out of her socket. "When the hell did you get this shit? What is that? Is that a snake?!"

He punched her in the back of the head and she curled up in a ball. Her daddy's fury made Henry and Heinrich take a step back.

"Are you trying to make me look bad?!" her daddy shouted as he punched her again.

Frankie lay on the bed curled into a ball with her hands covering her head and her knees drawn up to her chest. She closed her eyes and tried to place her mind elsewhere as another punch landed on her back. The punches stopped for a moment as her daddy removed his belt and wrapped the end of it around his hand. The first strike cracked against her back and opened up her skin and her eyes bolted open. She screamed involuntarily, but she wouldn't beg. There had been a shift in her mind: I will either die, she thought, or this will never happen again. The pressure in her mind was still building.

Her daddy grabbed her and pulled her off the bed, choking her and slamming her back against the wardrobe. Frankie looked deep into her daddy's eyes. He looked beyond her, maybe to a life without her, maybe to nothing, and tightened his grip on her throat.

The bedroom was growing darker, as though the day had already retired and night had begun. When Frankie looked beyond her daddy to the dirty window, it looked black outside.

The blackness shifted, she noticed. It wasn't night at all. Something was covering the window.

Then they entered the trailer.

Creatures poured in like black liquid through a broken section of the window and seeped up through the broken floorboards as if the trailer was suddenly drowned in a lake of tar.

"What the hell?!" Heinrich shouted as he was swarmed in insects and spiders.

Frankie was suffocating under her daddy's grip. Her vision was failing. Her muscles were becoming limp. Her hearing was becoming distorted, as if she was being submerged. But the whispering she had heard earlier was back.

It was a million small voices, all saying her name. She opened her eyes and tried to speak to them. Though she didn't have the strength to speak, they heard her cries.

The black tar that was filling the trailer started to break off into thousands of little shapes. There were spiders of a hundred varieties – house spiders, money spiders, daddy long legs – and a plethora of insects – black beetles, grasshoppers, cockroaches. A carpet of small snakes and large centipedes writhed around their feet and rose, wrapping themselves around the men. Frankie's fear overpowered her anger and she felt only joy at seeing them.

Frankie's daddy dropped her and she fell to the floor with her back to the wall as he tried in vain to brush off hundreds of insects that were crawling up his legs and into his clothes. He started screaming as he felt their legs tickling his body all over and began hitting himself to squash them.

"What the hell is going on?!" he screamed.

Frankie covered her mouth in shock.

"Get 'em off me!" Heinrich shouted, waving his arms and his shotgun all around in a blind panic. "Get 'em off me!"

"Stand-" Henry began, reaching for his brother, before a deafening blast of the shotgun cut Henry's sentence off along with the top half of his skull which exploded against the wall as Heinrich's finger brushed the trigger.

"Oh, God!" Heinrich shouted as Henry's corpse dropped into the tide of small insects. Heinrich lifted his gun and fired into a gap in the floorboards where long, brown swamp snakes were swarming through. "You little bastards!" he shouted. He began screaming as they lunged and bit into his legs and crotch.

After a few moments of shock, Frankie, untouched by the insects and the snakes, removed her hand from her mouth to reveal a smile. She stood up.

Heinrich fell to the floor next to the half-headless corpse of his brother. He dropped the shotgun and started writhing in agony and flapping his arms as he was bitten by a hundred snakes and stung by a thousand tiny spider bites. There were no poisonous creatures, for that's the way Frankie wanted it. Heinrich screamed and his eyes locked on Frankie as inch-by-inch his body was nipped away and his blood merged with the black tide of the dark and low creatures.

"Help me!" he shouted to Frankie. "Do something!"

Frankie waved both hands as if conducting an orchestra and the insects and the snakes scattered away from Heinrich, parting and exposing his shredded flesh. Heinrich looked around in horror as the insects obeyed Frankie. She swirled her right hand and those to her right scurried in a spiral motion up and across the wall. Frankie laughed. Her daddy looked up at her in horror from his position on his knees on the floor as he fought off cockroaches and dragged them out of his mouth and covered his nose.

"I am doing something," Frankie said.

She looked at Heinrich and stopped smiling.

"I'm not afraid of you," she said.

She brought her hands together in a clap and the insects and the spiders and the snakes came together in a wave from either side which engulfed Heinrich. He screamed with a mouth filled with centipedes until a long green-and-brown striped snake slithered out of the pool of blood on the floor and curled around Heinrich's neck and pressed its head into his mouth. Heinrich pulled at the snake, but it was too slippery to hold. Its tail wriggled back and forth in time with horrific choking noises from Heinrich as the snake tunneled its way deep into his throat and down into his chest. Heinrich's face turned blue as the tail of the snake disappeared down his mouth and the house spiders followed. He screamed silently, crunching spiders between his teeth as he gasped for air that wouldn't come. He grabbed his face in agony and tore at his skin with his nails, despairing in his final moments, ripping chunks from himself until at last he stopped moving but for the pulsating of his stomach where the snake and the spiders and the centipedes were squirming within him.

Frankie's daddy had found respite as the creatures swarmed over Heinrich and he looked back to his daughter with bloody tears in his eyes, his face red with small bites, his legs bleeding with larger ones.

"I'm-" he stuttered, looking at her, "I'm your daddy. You don't got no-one else."

Frankie said nothing.

"I love you, Frankie," her daddy said, raising his hands to her to plead. "You're my girl."

Frankie felt her insides turn to jelly and her knees begin to give underneath her. It was everything she had always wanted to hear. One kind word, she thought. I would've taken one kind word from this man and I would've been happy.

How wrong I was, she thought.

"You're my girl," her daddy said.

"I'm not your girl!" Frankie screamed. "I'm not your anything!"

Frankie's daddy jumped to his feet and pushed Frankie aside, slamming her head into the wall, as he made for the door. Holding her head, Frankie followed. The snakes zig-zagged over the bloodied carpet and into the hallway after her daddy where they leaped up at his legs and tore chunks from his ankles, sending him sprawling on his face into the lounge area. Standing over him, Frankie moved the creatures aside with a swoop of her hand.

Her daddy turned and looked up at her. "Please!" he screamed.

Frankie moved her fingers thinking of what to bring forth, and Georgia's most dangerous of the darkest and lowest creatures presented themselves, pushing through the black tide and encircling her daddy.

First came the snakes: the dusty-colored rattlesnakes; the green cottonmouths; the deadly copperheads. They surrounded her daddy. Then came the spiders and the scorpions: the glistening black widows, as big as a human hand; the small-bodied and almost translucent brown recluses; the chunky, brown devil scorpions. They crawled into the center of the circle made by the snakes and attached themselves to her daddy's body, crawling up his pants and down his sleeves and clinging to his screaming, white face. As the pincers closed around his skin and the scorpion's daggers penetrated his body, her daddy begged for his life in garbled, half-formed words as his bloodstream was overcome with poison that burned him from the inside out. When the snakes began to strike, they went for his face and genitals, popping his testicles and one of his eyeballs. Frankie raised her hands once more and the floorboards cracked and snapped upwards as she summoned the oldest of the low creatures. Three grinning alligators emerged from the darkness under the floorboards, pulling themselves through with small, powerful arms and propelling themselves with slashes of their long, thick tails. When her daddy saw the alligators, he emitted a single scream that lasted from the moment they arrived to the moment of his death. His scream was distorted and broken off by the jaws of the alligators around his head and body as they span and thrashed and broke every bone in his body, but it returned spasmodically as his body returned to something approaching its normal position for a split-second in between being twisted and pulverized by rows upon rows of razor-sharp teeth.

Frankie's father and his attackers became a nightmarish biomass on the floor, a thrashing, writhing, screaming and roaring collective of nature and humanity.

Within moments, the beating heart of the biomass, Frankie's horrified, tortured father, stopped moving. The creatures continued their feast and Frankie sat on the floor amidst them.

She was no longer afraid of any creature the earth could produce.

She tucked her knees up to her chest and rested her chin on her folded arms. She closed her eyes and wished for nothing further other than to disappear forever. She could feel it happening as she rested. A silk blanket was engulfing her, growing around her as the spiders worked to produce for her a cocoon. She opened her eyes and the darkness was complete. She was wrapped from head-to-toe in spider-webs. Rolling onto her side, she began to cry.

No library books could stop it.

No trips to the playground could distract her from it.

No mix-tapes could shut out her thoughts.

She was no longer afraid of any creature the earth could produce, apart from one – men – and she no longer wanted to live in place with such creatures.

The crocodiles and the snakes and the spiders and the scorpions worked as one and Frankie felt herself being pulled away from the world in her cocoon. Out of the trailer and into the woods and off to the wild nothing beyond.

She didn't know where they were dragging her. Frankie knew there was no place good to go to on this Earth.

Maybe they'll take me below it, she thought, where my mom is.

Maybe down there is better.

The End.

THE LAST VICTIM

SEAN PORTER

Chapter One

In all the world, I am the best at what I do.

Maybe some people don't consider what I do all that important. I'm not a doctor. I've never discovered the cure for any life-threatening diseases. I'm never going to write the great American novel. My name will most likely never be found in the footnotes of a history book.

What I do, is find people.

At this particular moment, I'm finding a man hiding in this out of town motel off County Road Seven. Just eight rooms out here and the guy I'm looking for is in number three. Been there for a week, dodging the police.

My business cards read Private Investigator. My business license for the state says that I'm a self-employed investigations specialist. People who hire me call me a problem solver.

I find people. I've dedicated my life to finding the bad people who don't want to be found. Like Martin Cassuk here in room three.

Very few people actually know my name. I get references from friends of friends who know me as Arthur, and Arthur's as good a name as any. It's a name that blends in and doesn't stand out. Like me. Light brown hair that's not long or short. A physique that's trim but not bulky with muscles. I'm average height, average looks, average everything. The only thing about me that stands out is the striking blue color of my eyes, but most of the times when someone gets close enough to get a good look at them, it's when it's too late to get away.

I've been hired by the police, on occasion, but they pay their checks to an Arthur Murray with a bank account that isn't actually attached to anything except that name. If you aren't sure who Arthur Murray is, look him up. The irony of it goes over most people's heads. I laugh whenever I cash my checks.

Mostly, private individuals hire me. I choose my jobs very carefully. I'm not ever going to work a job that requires me to kidnap an innocent person. Never going to commit a felony or a Federal offense—not without a good reason. If your child is missing, call me and I can find them. If your ex skipped town rather than pay child support, I can find them. If a person has five outstanding warrants for assault and attempted murder and they think they can hide in a third-rate motel off County Road Seven, then I'm the guy who's going to find him.

Not just find him. Take him into custody, and bring him to justice.

Because I'm the best there is at what I do.

The guy working the front counter for the motel is more than agreeable to take the couple hundred bucks I give him to go away for an hour. There's a few other guests in the motel, but so long as none of them poke their heads out to see what the problem is, then they'll be fine. I only need a few minutes.

Room three had the blinds drawn. For most people who are hiding out, it's a way for them to hide from the world. What people tend to forget is that if I can't see in, they can't see out either. Which means I get to stroll up to the door of Martin's motel room without him even knowing.

A shape charge is a small amount of C4 tucked into a half-circle of either metal or ceramic which directs the blast force forward. Put one of those on or near the handle of a locked door and it will pretty much make splinters of the whole locking mechanism. It will also make a loud enough noise to draw the attention of anyone within a half-mile radius.

The easiest way to get through a locked door is to simply put all of your weight on the back foot and then kick straight forward with your other, smashing your heel into the door right by the door handle. It makes a little bit of a racket, but nowhere near as much as a small controlled explosion.

As the door banged open against the inside wall I burst in fast and furious. I've learned from any number of mistakes that going in politely and asking someone to just give up only gets you hurt. Badly.

Martin is sitting on one of the beds watching a game show on the tiny television set when I came crashing down on him. There are any number of military-style fighting techniques that can subdue a man in under a minute. I prefer a sort of blitzkrieg attack. Unload everything before the other person has a chance to even realize they're in trouble.

This guy is twice my size, and he's not a really nice person, but I have him down on the floor and bleeding from his mouth and nose in short order. With my knee in his back, I fold his one arm around behind him and start to hook my handcuffs in place.

"Don't feel bad," I tell him. "I've taken down tougher guys than—"

He bucked like a damned bull and threw me off his back, tumbling me to the floor and putting me into an ankle lock. "You ain't never dealt with somebody as tough as me."

Holding someone's ankle backward is painful, but it only really holds someone pinned down in those stupid fake wrestling shows. All I needed to do was scissor kick my legs and the steel toes of the boot on my free foot are breaking Martin's jaw. It doesn't matter how much you want to fight someone, once your jaw gets broken the pain keeps you from doing anything except gurgling hysterically and trying to hold your face together.

After that, it was a simple matter to handcuff Martin and lead him out to my waiting car. He was a lot more humble as I put him in the back seat. The doors lock from the inside but I doubt I'll have to worry about this man trying to jump out of my car and get away. He's barely staying conscious now as it is.

Smiling, I slammed my door shut and started the engine. "Try not to bleed too much on my upholstery," I tell him. "And don't worry about your jaw. The prison you're going to has great doctors."

In the rearview mirror, I can see Martin slumping against the seat. He's already passed out.

Chapter Two

So you've got to be wondering what type of person goes into people-finding as a profession. The money's good but that's only part of it. I know a lot of the people in this profession. Most of them—of us, I should say—have one thing in common. Somewhere in our pasts, something went horribly wrong.

For me, it was my sister.

When I was eighteen years old, Cindy was already twenty-one. Every night I see the moment when my sister was murdered in my dreams. I wasn't there, and there's no way I could know the gruesome details that get packed into my dreams, but I see it just the same. Her body being slashed, her blood running down her perfect skin, and a man's dark shadow standing over her and laughing with glee. It keeps the raw emotions fresh and hurting.

Cindy was so smart and so pretty. She had the world wrapped around her fingers. Everything came easy to her. Anything she wanted she got, through effort and hard work. I loved my sister.

Then she took up with a man who ruined her life.

Kirk Danes was wrong for Cindy right from the start. A slick man who liked to wear button-up shirts under a leather jacket. No job. No future. Yet my sister fell head over heels for him. I tried to warn her. I tried to tell her he was trouble. She wouldn't listen to me or anyone else.

The night he murdered her was supposed to be the night of my prom. I never went to that dance. I've never been to any dance since.

Cindy's body was never found. Just her blood spilled across her bed and her torn dress laying next to it. Kirk Danes was never found, either. The man who killed my sister was gone.

I've spent my entire life since then looking for him. I'm twenty-eight now. That's a lot of years to carry a grudge.

The skills I've learned looking for this man are what developed into my current career. It's what made me so good at finding people and bringing them to justice in whatever form that might take. There's no place on Earth that anyone can hide from me. I've never once taken on a job and failed to find the mark.

That doesn't make up for the fact that I can't find Kirk Danes. I've turned over every rock I can think of but he's just nowhere to be found. There's no trace of the man. At least, not yet.

My apartment isn't big. It's enough for me and myself. The kitchen is part of the dining room and the living room is spacious and lined with bookshelves and the bathroom is just as large as the one bedroom at the end of the hall. It's mine. It's where I live, and it's where I prepare for my jobs. I sit here on the couch like this and spread out my folders and study up on my target.

Kirk's folders are pretty thick. I know where he grew up, where he was living, every single place that he ever worked. I know his friends and known associates and his only two living relatives. I knew where he did his banking—twenty dollars and thirteen cents in savings—and who he owed money to. I even found the other women he murdered across the United States and Canada. Seven in all, including my sister. She was just one more in a long string of bodies for Kirk Danes, serial killer.

There have been others since. Oh yeah, I've found his latest kills. It's a matter of matching up the little things, like the torn dresses, a body that gets moved from the scene only to be found months or years later, the way he...does things to them before he kills them. Two of the current victims haven't been found yet, either. Just like my sister. But I know it's him. My instincts like this are never wrong. All of these women were killed by Kirk Danes. I know what he likes.

I know everything about the man. Except where he was right now at this moment.

I threw my pen down at the tabletop only to have it bounce off the pages in the folder and land on the floor on the opposite side. Whatever. I obviously wasn't going to get anywhere with the folders again today. The paycheck for taking in Martin Cassuk had been deposited earlier in the day and I was flush again. Maybe it was time to go out and do something. Have some fun. Take my mind off the impossible.

As if that would ever happen. I can't forget my sister. I will never forget what was done to her, and I will bring Kirk to justice.

Just not tonight. If I couldn't nail Kirk to the nearest wall tonight, then I might as well go out and do something. The night is young, and so am I. There's a nightclub down the street that I like to hang out in sometimes. The music is loud and innocuous, but there's always groups of women there who are looking for a man to spend time with and forget their own troubles. My last hookup from there was Jennifer. Now that had been a night where I nearly forgot about my sister. Jennifer had a way of making a man forget anything except her. If she was there again tonight that would so make it worth my while to go out...

My hands hesitated as they put together the piles of paperwork together. This one page. I've looked at this one-page dozens of times and I could probably recite all the information on it by heart. So why had I never noticed this before?

One of Kirk's known associates was a woman by the name of Erika Barton. She had a history of being in and out of court-ordered drug rehabs. Which meant she got arrested for drug crimes a lot. Want to find a drug addict who gets arrested a lot, you talk to the police. If I want to know where Kirk Danes might be now, I need to find Erika Barton and make her talk. If I can make that happen I can come at him sideways.

I know just the guy to help me find her.

Granted it's late. After eleven o'clock, actually, but the law enforcement profession is a twenty-four-hour business. And yes, a guy in my line of work has contacts in the police. You need to if you're going to keep two steps ahead of the bad guys. Actually, the police are usually one step behind the criminals, but add in my intelligence and skillset and that puts me ahead of the curve. The police come to me when they can't find someone, after all.

The phone rings three times before my friend Barney answers. Barney's a sergeant with the state police. All business, usually, until you take the man out for a beer or two and get him talking. Then he'll tell you every little detail of his life. Or enough of it to let out some sensitive information he'd rather not have anyone else know. I promised never to tell, as long as I get a favor or two from time to time.

In other words, he owes me.

"What in the hell do you want?" is how he answers the phone.

"Now is that any way to treat an old friend?" I say with a smile. Even though he can't see it, he'll still hear it in my voice. "I need a favor. I need to know where a girl by the name of Erika Barton is right now."

I have him Barton's information, her date of birth and her soc number and everything else I could, and then listened to him swear at me about how he was going to get his ass in a sling for helping me. I knew he wasn't, and he knew he wasn't, but it made Barney feel better to complain about it, so I let him complain.

A few dozen keystrokes and five minutes later, he had the information for me that I needed about where to find Erika. I thanked him and was about to hang up when he told me there was more.

"Got a body today."

"Good for you," I quipped. "She your type?"

"Ha, ha. This body might interest you, actually."

"No, thanks. I'm already in a relationship."

"You'll make an exception." He waited for someone on his end of the line to move away before he added, "This body was killed in the same way the others were."

"Where?" I said immediately, nearly diving over the table to collect the pen I'd tossed away before. I needed this address. There's one more detail about the Kirk Danes murders that I've never told anyone. This piece of information I've saved for myself.

Whenever he kills, he always returns to the scene of the murder within twenty-four hours. It's his way of getting his kicks. Of showing the police that he's better than they are. Untouchable. Unstoppable. Like he's giving them the finger.

Or maybe he just likes to jack off where he kills the girls.

Whatever his reason, he'll be back at the scene of this newest murder soon. I'll be there to stop him.

Chapter Three

Abandoned warehouses are kind of like weeds on your lawn. You never notice them until you go looking, and then they're everywhere.

The one I'm in was used by a Chinese wholesale food store in its past life. Now it's just big empty rooms with a catwalk hanging on the side of the wall halfway up to the ceiling, looking down over everything. Makes for the perfect perch to watch, and wait.

The police tape is still up around a square spot on the cement floor down below. The body has been removed, of course. This is the way Kirk Danes likes it. The police are out busy looking for him. Now he's going to be here where he can enjoy the aftermath of his handiwork without being disturbed.

Not that the man isn't disturbed enough as it is.

In black clothes and a long black coat, I have myself huddled into a corner and watching everything with a pair of night-vision goggles. It's already one in the morning, and my time frame for Kirk showing up to marvel at his handiwork is running out. I hope I haven't missed him. If he got here before I did and he's already gone again—

There. Down there in the moonlight coming in from the only window in this room. The dust motes stirred as a shadow slipped past. There's my guy. Serial killer Kirk Danes. The man who killed my sister.

From under my coat, I take the long-barreled pistol I use for this kind of work. There's no silencer on it. Doesn't need to be, when the gun fires tranq darts. Let the guy sleep his way to a jail cell. I'm good with that.

What I want to do is tear him apart limb from limb but that won't get my sister justice. I have to remember my goal here. Capture and interrogation. I want to know why he did this to my sister.

I level the gun out on the railing, aiming down at the shadow that I can still see moving thanks to my night-vision goggles. Hard to make out any specifics in the gloom. Tall, maybe. Thin, but he's wearing a coat sort of like mine that disguises him pretty well.

There. He's stopped. Every criminal as sick as this guy has to admire their work. It's like some damned law of nature. So just stand there, you son-of-a-bitch, and take your medicine.

A bright flash centered on the guy below me lights up my goggles and momentarily blinds me. It's only my razor-quick reflexes that make me react by throwing myself backward, flat against the catwalk, making myself as small a target as I can.

Good thing, too. Around me, the cement wall sparks and chips as multiple bullets strike one after the other. That's the sound of an automatic weapon. All speed, no accuracy, even in the hands of an expert. Kirk knew enough to flash a light and blind me before opening fire. That's the mark of a pro.

Guess when you kill a dozen women or more over your serial killer career you learn a certain skill set of your own.

Crawling along the catwalk, trying to get out of the range of the bullets as they follow me, I have two different thoughts run through my mind. One, I can't underestimate Kirk Danes again. No more considering him just a psychopathic maniac. This guy's dangerous.

Two, I really wish I'd brought something other than a tranq gun with me.

The catwalk came to an abrupt end at a corner and when I tried to make the turn a hail of bullets rained down against the wall and careened off the metal of the walkway. I was trapped, and I was dead if I didn't come up with something.

In desperation, I pointed the tranq gun and fired off the entire clip of ten shots. They're ballistically propelled which means each one sounds like a gunshot. All the bang, none of the lethal impact.

When the gun clicked empty I sat there, waiting to die.

Silence met me, mixing with the oily stink of my own fear. I dared a glance over the railing.

The room was empty. Kirk Danes was gone.

In the darkness, I swore very loudly, and very descriptively. This was my chance. Maybe my one and only chance to grab this guy and I blew it. There was nothing for me to do except pack up, go home, and regroup.

Well. I still had the address of his known associate. And hey, it was a brand new day. I haven't gotten any sleep and I haven't had anything to eat in the last fifteen hours, but why stop now?

I know this much. I'm getting my gun before I go any further.

My car is parked a few blocks over from the warehouse. Five minutes of walking gets me there, and the engine purrs under the hood as I pull out and head for the next intersection. It's going to take me twenty minutes or better to get to Erika Barton's apartment but on the plus side, she won't be expecting me there at this hour. I'll have the element of surprise on my side, just like I thought I'd have it back in the warehouse.

As I'm driving I take out my forty-caliber Desert Eagle from my glove compartment. The weight of it feels good in my hand. Holding it up to examine it in the light from the guy behind me I make sure the safety's off. This time, I mean business.

The lights from the car following me get closer. I can see them reflecting brighter off the burnished metal sides of my semi-automatic.

A second before my brain registers what that means, I hear the rev of an engine. The car behind me isn't just following. It's trying to catch up.

It's bumper tags mine, and I accelerate to keep distance between us.

"Bastard," I mutter. "You run out of bullets or what?"

Kirk Danes is behind me. He's trying to kill me. Again.

My car doesn't look like much but it has as much horsepower and torque as anything on the road. Those are the two things that measure the power of a vehicle. It's what allows me to take a turn against the light at a nearly ninety-degree angle and then keep going as Kirk's car squeals straight through the intersection, unable to stop in time.

Take that, you bastard.

Thankfully, it's late enough at night that there aren't that many police patrols around. Not that much traffic either, at least not in this section of town. In the empty street, with nothing but the neon from closed businesses to see me, I brake hard and twist the wheel and spin one-hundred-eighty degrees so that I'm facing back the way I just came. Smoke rolls off my tires. The noise echoes down the alleyways.

Kirk's car backs slowly up into the intersection and then turns to face me. He revs his engine a few times. I do the same.

That's macho talk for come and get me.

With a shriek of burning rubber, Kirk's car races at me. I can only see his shadow behind the wheel but that's all I need.

In medieval times knights used to joust each other with long pointed sticks. They would ride at each other just as fast as they could and try to land a blow against the other knight first. Well. I don't have a pointed stick. I do have a Desert Eagle.

Pushing the automatic down button on my window I take my gun in my left hand, my off hand, and fire ten rounds straight into Kirk's windshield. His car veers off to jump the curb and crash through a bus stop shelter.

Then he's veering back at me and shooting through the blown out windshield with his full auto machine pistol.

One of the bullets zips across my right shoulder as I turn the wheel frantically, trying to save my life. He was still alive. How was he still alive?

I raced down the street, taking turns at random, trying to lose the maniac driving up my tailpipe. It was painfully obvious that Kirk had no regard for his own life. People who wanted to live didn't risk their own lives to kill someone else. My car jolted and rocked as he rammed my bumper again and again. I barely kept it on the road when he sped up to hit me in an alley I'd ducked down to use as an escape path. My passenger side careened against the brick wall of a business and then we were out the other side and I could hear the disturbing sounds of a flat tire as my car began listing to the right.

When you're being pursued by another vehicle, you have two choices if you can't get away. One is to take the chase into a well-populated area. Unfortunately, that means getting civilians involved and possible killed. Not an option for me.

The other is to terminate the pursuit and deal with the consequences.

Like this.

Slamming on the brakes just as hard as I could, bracing myself for what would come next, I intentionally crashed the backend of my car into the speeding front end of Kirk's. It made a horrendous noise, and his car was vaulted up on top of mine. The impact sent me bouncing forward and my head cracked against the steering wheel. Darkness threatened to overtake me as our mangled cars came to a combined stop. I knew if I gave in, I'd be dead.

If anyone was going to die today it was going to be Kirk. Not me.

Forcing myself to move, I got my door open as far as the warped metal would go, and then made sure my gun was still in my hand as I walked back to where Kirk's door stood already open. His car was empty. A blood trail led off down the street, and as I looked around I could see where we were, and my fuzzy, muddled brain suddenly clued into exactly where Kirk was going.

We were very close to where Erika Barton's apartment was.

The sirens were already coming. I wasn't going to be in a position to answer questions until I had Kirk in hand, in custody, as the punchline to anything I was going to say.

So I ran. This was getting real. I was marked for death by a serial killer but if I wasn't going to live to see daybreak, then neither was he.

Chapter Four

In the apartment hallway, I moved one step at a time, staying close to the wall. This was a grimy, rundown apartment building. The third floor here looked just like every other hall and if it wasn't for the numbers tacked with small nails to each door I would never have known which one was apartment twelve.

When I got to it, I made myself stand there for several long moments and listen. Inside I could hear voices. They were low and muffled but there was definitely two of them. Guess even a creep like Kirk needs someone to help him sometimes.

My shoulder hurt, and my head was still throbbing, and there was this ache in my ribs I couldn't quite remember getting but I know it hurt. I didn't care. This was for my sister. I wasn't going to give up, no matter what.

I couldn't just crash through this door with my boot. With Kirk right on the other side, I needed stealth. Everyone in the trade worth their salt carries a lock pick set with them. Mine is made from stainless steel. The torsion wrench slid in silently, while the rake made soft clicking noises as it went into the plug. A steady hand and experience had the single lock on the door open in less than sixty seconds. Then all I had to do was ease the door open and slip inside.

The short entryway led to a wide open living room, kitchen, and dining room combined. Clothes were thrown everywhere. Half-empty Chinese food cartons were tipped over on the coffee table and piled up high in the garbage can. I swept my gun left, and then right, and found no one. There were doors leading off these rooms. Kirk must have gone into one of those. For now, I had the element of surprise.

One of these doors was a bathroom. One of them was a bedroom. Maybe even a closet. Damn. I hate doors.

My initial idea is to stay right here, where I can see all the doors at once. Eventually, Kirk and his friend Erika are going to have to come out of whatever hiding place they've slid into. When they came out, here I'd be, waiting.

There's the door to the left. The one in front of me. The one to the right...

When the door in front of me began blowing apart to the sound of distant thunder it was too late. Bullets, raining down sideways at me with the speed of thought. One struck my leg and shoved it out from under me. I fell flat on my face, my gun hand hitting hard and stinging. It was a miracle I managed to hold onto the weapon.

It was another miracle none of the other bullets hit me. The one that was now lodged in the muscle of my thigh had saved my life by knocking me to the floor. I got my breath again and aimed at the door. I couldn't take the shot. There was someone else in this apartment because I'd heard another voice and it was probably Erika and I couldn't just shoot. If I killed her at the same time I'd have a hell of a time explaining it to the police after.

One last bullet made a hole in the door. Then it started to open.

I got to my knees. Then I got to my feet, keeping the weight off my injured leg, and leveled the gun at the person emerging from the darkness beyond the door. My finger tensed on the trigger.

It was a woman. Someone I'd never seen before. She was thin and leggy and her long black hair was tied up at the back of her neck. Her eyes were wide with fear. The necklace at her throat caught the light.

No. It wasn't a necklace. I saw it better as she stepped out more. It was a knife. The blade of it was pointed in toward her skin, held in the fist of the person behind her.

Erika wasn't Kirks associate anymore. Now she was a human shield.

"Kirk," I said very slowly, very purposefully. "Get your ass out here and stop hiding behind her."

They took a step closer to me, and now I saw the same shadowy figure in the long, hooded coat that I've been chasing all over town. I've got a gun, he's got a knife, and sure that gives me an edge...if I'm willing to shoot through someone to kill him. I want to kill him. I really, really do. My emotions are all torn up knowing the man who murdered my sister is standing right there waiting to receive his final justice. My body is hurt and broken and I can feel my stamina flagging. I should take the shot right now and end all this.

But I won't kill an innocent person. That's not who I am. That's not who my sister would want me to be.

So, for the sake of Cindy's memory, I use the other weapon at my disposal. I keep talking.

"Let her go, Kirk, and lets you and me discuss this man to man. You know who I am?"

From the shadows within the hood, I hear soft, hissing laughter.

"Yeah," I tell him, my hand tightening on the grip of my gun. "You know who I am. I'm the guy who's going to end you. I'm the guy who's been trailing you from state to state and then right back here to your home ground. I'm the guy whose sister you killed all those years ago."

When I take a step closer, his hand shoves the knife closer into Erika's neck. Close enough, I guess. I could probably put a bullet into that hood and kill him without killing Erika. Probably.

One last try at making nice. "Make your choice, you bastard, because this stops today."

Then Kirk looked up at me, and the hood fell back.

That smile didn't belong to Kirk Danes. This was a woman. It had been years since I saw her pretty face, but I recognized her right away. My blood turned to ice. I swear my heart stopped when I realized what I was seeing.

Who. When I realized who I was seeing.

Cindy. My sister.

"Hey there, bro," she told me. "About time you figured things out."

"You're...dead." The words sounded stupid in my ears. Things were already starting to fall into place. If this wasn't Kirk that I've been tracing, if it was my sister, then all those victims...all those dead girls...the serial killer I've traced for years was her.

Slowly, Cindy drew the knife gently across Erika's cheek. It drew a line of blood as my sister laughed. "Of course, I'm not dead, brother dear. I've been living. This is the most alive that I've ever been."

My gun had dropped and now I reset the aim on my sister. She can't be here. There's no way. She's dead. She's dead, damn it, she's dead! Only...no, she's not. She's here, holding a woman hostage. My sister, risen from the dead. "Cindy, let her go. Please, let her go. Let's talk about—"

She plunged the knife into the side of Erika's throat as I stood there watching. Blood sprayed. Erika's scream turned into a gurgle and she crumpled to the floor kicking and dying.

And I pulled the trigger on my gun.

I couldn't call the bullet back, as much as I wanted to. Here I stood, bleeding and injured by Cindy herself, looking at a person who was responsible for deaths on a double-digit scale, and I wanted to throw myself in the path of the bullet that was surely going to kill her.

In the next instant, Cindy was thrown backward into the room behind her. She was dead. None of this made any sense and now...I'd never get a chance to ask her why she was alive. Why she was killing people. Why she'd tried to kill me.

I fell to my knees. The tears were unexpected, hot with emotion, and uncontrollable. There was no part of me that didn't hurt. Outside, or in. The gun in my hand felt too heavy, and too hot, and somehow evil. I tossed it aside. I didn't want it anymore. My whole life had been a lie. Everything I've ever believed or ever done has been based on a lie. When would the room stop spinning?

I was going to throw up all over the floor but I needed to get out of here. That shot was going to draw the attention of at least a few of the tenants and then they would call the police and I did not want to try explaining this to anyone else right now. I didn't even understand it myself.

The scream that filled the room brought my attention up and sent burning cold racing up my spine. The heavyweight barreling into me put me flat on the floor. Arms wrapped around my neck, choking off my air.

"You're a real bastard," Cindy hissed in my ear. "You and Mom and Dad were part of why I disappeared. Did you know that? Of course not. You were clueless. Thought we were best friends or something."

I couldn't get my fingers in behind her arm to pry it away. What the hell was I supposed to do here? Flopping her over so she was on her back below me was the best I could manage. She was still choking me. She was still trying to kill me.

"I had to fake my own damned death," she told me, her voice bitter. "I had to find the right patsy to date. A guy who the police already suspected of being a criminal. I had to lead him on and fuck him senseless just to get him to stay with me until I could fake my death. I stored my blood and threw it around the room and then I had to kill him and drop his body down...well. That's a secret."

I rolled to my side. No good. Still dying. My fingernails scrabbled at the floor trying to get enough purchase to crawl away.

"Oh, no no no," Cindy told me. "You don't get away. You die, brother dear. You die. Just like all these skank women who had to die. They all screwed the wrong guys. Like the first one. She took my boyfriend, and I killed her. I killed her, and the next one, and the next one, and I'll kill every damned one that I find until it stops!"

My hand hit something hard. Something cold and metallic.

"You should have left me alone," Cindy said, squeezing harder until stars were popping in front of my eyes. "It was hard to stay away from you. I had to duck my own brother to keep my secret. All this time you thought I was Kirk Danes. Idiot. It was me. Always me."

I caught hold of my Desert Eagle's handle. I picked it up, and turned it around and fired.

The bullet went through my shoulder, and into Cindy's chest. I felt my bones shattering as I finally lost consciousness and passed out.

Chapter Five

The papers called me a hero.

Heroes shouldn't cry. Or drink themselves to sleep every night.

I'm the best at what I do. Even with one working arm. The bullet had found my sister's heart. Killed her instantly.

What Cindy did to me shattered my heart as surely as any bullet would have. I have to keep living, though. I don't get to die.

Not today.

MISTER SLASHER

DUKE MORRISON

John looked out at the kids on the school campus. He had been going to the same school for a few years and it was sickening to see all of them were generally the same. His friends were an odd bunch, with their own special part making them a unique group. Juice, or Jack but they called him Juice, was really good at getting any type of drug the group wanted. Jonk, or Rachel, was more of a book and nerdy type, but she always had money, which came in handy when they were trying to enjoy themselves. Janice was a bit over the top with her weapon's fanaticism and she really liked to cosplay.

John was the muscle of their group and was usually the one people had to contend with if they wanted to pick on Juice or Janice. That suited him just fine because it gave him a good excuse to find and use the martial arts that he had dedicated himself to learning over the years.

"John, you'll never believe this." Juice called out to John as he headed over to his car.

"I'm gonna go out on a limb here and say we're going to have a good weekend," John said as Juice got into the passenger seat.

"Hell yeah. I just found a dealer that's willing to sell us a pound for twenty bucks provided we're the ones picking the buds." Juice said.

John raised his eyebrow. That sounded like a deal and it wasn't uncommon to find dealers who were too lazy to pick their own crop. However, Juice was not usually one to travel out of town for any type of product.

"What makes it so special that we need to go in on this deal?" John asked.

Juice smiled.

"Gold Thinker, my friend. It's a farm of Girl Scout Cookies and Kosher Kush." Juice said excitedly.

"Um... aren't those two usually one hundred bucks a gram?" John asked, even more suspicious now that he knew what it was.

"That's the great part. Apparently, the guy offers the price to people who want to hang out with him for a few hours. It's a literal pot buffet, and the only price to pay is a few bucks and some time with a man who is probably baked with tons munchies. He goes by the name Mr. Slasher." Juice said.

"That's an odd name," Janice said as she hopped into the back of the car.

"Well, not really. He says he's possessed by a murderer who used to call himself Mr. Slasher." Juice said nonchalantly as he ruffled through his backpack for something.

"No offense, Juice, but I'm not particularly crazy about visiting a man who says he's possessed by a murderer." John pointed out.

"Oh please, it's not like he's an actual murderer. I did a background check on the man after I had one of my friends look on his computer. The man is completely free of all crimes we know of in this country. He probably just says that so that people who murder over this type of stuff think twice before coming to his place. After all, all he really wants to do is sit back and chill with a few people. He's got a home theater and everything." Juice said.

"You found out about him how?" Janice questioned.

"A friend who went there himself and lost himself for a couple of months. I figured since this was the end of the school year, that we would go down and lose ourselves for a couple of months too. To be honest, this sounds like the deal of a lifetime. Do you think that Jonk would be able to afford the trip?" Juice asked.

"Juice, how many times have I told you not to question how much money I have? I'd have to kill you if I ever told you." Jonk said, slapping him on the back of the head.

"Woah!" John said, jumping slightly because he was surprised he didn't notice her come in.

"Did I scare you, John?" Jonk said, mischievously smiling.

The four of them hadn't met in your normal ways because they were each weird in their own way. John had originally met Juice first because he was a rebelling teenager that was looking for a good time with the rest of his buddies from his Dojo. Juice was the one who pulled him out of a bad cocaine deal that the rest of his buddies fell for, which is why John was not in prison. The two of them had known each other from middle school days and it wasn't until they got into high school that they had met the other two.

Janice was someone he had met through training because martial arts wouldn't be very martial without some type of weapons training. The Dojo had two separate classes, people who wanted to specialize in fighting with their hands and people who wanted to specialize with weaponry. The police force incorporated their people into both classes, which is why Janice was enrolled in the same Dojo as he was. The only difference is that he preferred to hear the skull crack underneath his fist and she preferred to get girly over how many times a piece of steel had been folded over to increase its strength.

The last one was actually quite amusing because each of them were not the best of students at school, primarily because they enjoyed their hobbies a lot more than they enjoyed their teachers. Therefore, each of them had a tutor for the subjects they were failing in that had been paid by their parents or rather each of them had the same tutor; Jonk. Jonk was brilliant and had technically already graduated whenever they had first met in their freshman year, so it wasn't entirely surprising that Jonk didn't actually attend any of the classes. The problem with the school is that they had no form of early graduation for students like Jonk. Since it was a rigid school, all tests, homework, and quizzes were the same as a means of standardization. Jonk had done four years worth of work in just a few months but she had to wait three more years after that to graduate. She used the extra time to charge for tutoring during everybody's free period.

"Alright, so where do we need to go then?" John asked.

"Well, we're here in Coleville and we need to go to Lost Cannon Peak. That's where this man's farm is." Juice said.

"So, we're going to drive like thirty minutes and then hike the rest of the way?" Jonk asked.

"Actually, that's very close to the Marine Corps Mountain Training Camp. We'll just travel there and head up to the peak." Janice pointed out.

"That's what I asked," Jonk said.

"No, we won't need to hike. There's a dirt trail up from the camp so we'll be able to drive up most of the way to him. After that, we should be practically there." Janice said.

"Oh, that's good. I don't particularly feel like walking through a bunch of forests just for a good time." John said, "However, we should probably bring along a bunch of food because I doubt there's a lot of places to get food where we are going."

"Where did you say this place was?" John asked as they went up the side of the mountain.

"It should be up this side of the dirt road." Juice said, looking down at the map.

"We've been out here for an hour," Jonk stated, rather displeased.

"Hey guys, I don't think we're going to see a house on the side of the road," Janice said, as she pointed out of the window.

The group changed their focus to where she was pointing and saw what looked like a massive log cabin that stood somewhere around an hour's walk from the road.

"If that's the house, you think he has a..."

"LOOK OUT!" Juice yelled.

John swerved as he just barely grazed a truck that was parked on the side of the road. It wouldn't have taken out the car, but it would have at least taken out the left side light along with crushing in the metal had it made impact.

"Hell!" John yelled, as he suddenly stopped the car.

"What is wrong with this guy?" Janice asked.

"Well, you might be right Janice. He might not have a driveway. It would be expensive to make a new one and I don't think the people who keep this place safe would look too kindly on it." Jonk said.

"Whatever."

John slowly pulled over to the side of the road and the group got out of the car. Luckily, most of the food they had packed was inside of bags, but that meant they would need to carry it quite a ways before they reached their destination.

"I think we should leave the food here and just make sure that this is the place we need to be. If it is, then we can come back and get the food." John said.

The group made their way up the side of the mountain. The summer heat was usually terrible by itself but with the surrounding of the trees, it was actually rather pleasant for the team and they all joked, and laughed, their way up the side of the mountain. The trip didn't take long, but when they got up there, the mansion of a log cabin they had seen from the dirt road became evidently more massive. It looked as though someone had built a castle out of wood and just called it a log cabin out of sheer humbleness. It was also not the run-on-gasoline type too, as they could see the glint of the solar panels before they had even arrived at the place. There was a pool and it generally looked like something they might have found along the Beverly Hills had they drove around long enough.

John walked up to the door and knocked. The door itself looked as though a giant had made it, or something that a fan of RPG's had custom made because they liked Viking architecture. The group waited in silence as they peeked inside of the window to see if there was visible life inside of it.

"Hello?!" John called out.

"What?!" A gruff voice answered from the back.

The group traveled around the side of the mansion to see fields of growing plants and a small courtyard with plenty of areas to rest.

There was a massive man standing in the center of it and he actually did look as though he had killed someone in the past. He had a patch over his eye and plenty of scars on his back, but he kept wacking away at wooden blocks.

"Mr. Slasher?" John inquired cautiously.

"Yeah." The man said as he continued to slam down on the blocks of wood.

"We're here with Juice." John stated.

The man lowered the ax and turned around to look at the group. There was a long silence as he looked each of them over. Then he went back to chopping the wood.

"Umm..." John began, looking for words to try and start a conversation.

"If you want your weed, go grocery shopping in the fields just ahead. Remember, twenty bucks a pound." He said, ignoring the group as a whole.

"Hey, I thought you said your friend lost a couple of months up here," John whispered to Juice.

"If you don't mind, I'm working here. If you want some weed, go get it. If you don't, then leave. I have my time and my peace, and I rather like it spent baked." Mr. Slasher stated, "You can wait until I'm done to hang out, but I want to get this done."

John looked at Juice on clues for what to do, but Juice had already started to move with a small bag in hand. He had bolted towards the plants and left the group to fend for themselves. The man continued to chop away at the wood for a long while before he stood up and stretched.

"Ah! That feels good. There's no exercise that's more demanding than a downward chop with some resistance. It seems your friend has descended on my plants. How long are you all planning to stay?" Mr. Slasher asked.

"Well, if you don't mind, sir, we had planned to spend our summer here," John stated.

Mr. Slasher raised an eyebrow.

"That's a really long time. I usually get visitors for a couple of days. You're kids from one of the schools, aren't you?" He asked.

"Yes," Janice said defiantly.

"I ain't had me some kids for a while. The story about me is usually enough to scare off trespassers and children with weak limbs. Only the big and dumb tend to come my way." Mr. Slasher pointed out.

"Well, I can tell you that we're not dumb," John said with a slight smile.

"You are if you hear my story and still come. I'm possessed by a murderer and people still take up my offer." Mr. Slasher said.

"Well, we figured that you just had that story to scare off people."

"No." The man said bluntly.

John couldn't tell if the man was joking or if he really did think that he was a murderer but the group was there now and it didn't seem as though he had any intention of murdering anyone. Truth be told, the man had kinda reminded him of his grandfather when John was still a small child. He remembered that his grandfather always had a serious composure even when he had told a joke and it was difficult to tell when he was happy. This man had a similar look and feel. He wondered if it was due to what they needed to do in order to survive the wilderness that caused the seriousness and the lack of emotional empathy. He was pretty bad at empathy himself, but at least people knew when he was happy or sad.

"Hey, guys. I got about two pounds of it." Juice yelled as he came back into the clearing.

He was carrying what looked like a heavy satchel of brush and the smell of it was extreme, like that of curdling milk. Pot had a distinct smell to it and if you had smoked pot before, the smell would be delicious. If you hadn't, the smell would make you want to gag. The man seemed to know this as he looked at each one of them and saw Jonk convulsing slightly.

"So, you brought a newbie up here?" Mr. Slasher asked.

The three of them looked at the man and then looked at Jonk. Jonk bashfully smiled and bent her head down in slight shame.

"What? I've never smoked before. You guys just never noticed that I passed the joint without smoking it." Jonk said.

"What's wrong little lady? All of those commercials telling you weed was bad?" Mr. Slasher questioned mockingly.

"I don't care for it," Jonk said, slightly angered by the man.

"Juice, take out a bud and roll it." The man said, looking directly at Jonk.

"We don't have any snacks. We left them back at the car." Juice pointed out.

"You think I'd be smoking weed every day and not have munchies? I've got a few fridges inside." Mr. Slasher pointed out, "Now, roll it up."

"I don't think she wants any," John said.

Mr. Slasher came over to John and looked down at him, "She smokes or no one gets any."

"You can't do that."

"Oh, I believe that I can. Are we going to have a problem?" Mr. Slasher asked as a smile broke out across his face.

"No, it's okay guys. I'll smoke some." Jonk said nervously.

Mr. Slasher walked over to Jonk, who trembled underneath his shadow. Then, in a weird moment, he was no longer menacing when he bent down.

"You seem like the nerd of the group, so it's time to learn some interesting facts about the so-called bad pot. The only reason why it was made illegal is because the lumber company wanted to monopolize on the building trade. You see, weed is useful for all kinds of things and one of them was a building material that was better than wood. The Native Americans have used weed as a medicinal chill pill longer than we've known about it. This supposed devil drug has never killed anyone and I heard on the telly that it even helps people with cancer. It's not like the other drugs in the drug trade, which can make you peel off your skin or accidentally kill someone with a car. It's a drug of peace. Why do you think so many hippies used to smoke it?" Mr. Slasher said, smiling at her.

"Oh, well, I suppose it can't be that bad then. I always see them try it, but my family is very strict about drugs and what they can do to you." Jonk said.

"I know. Since parents have had kids, we've always had the overbearing parents. It takes other kids and parents to break them out of that habit." Mr. Slasher said as he rubbed her head.

"So, where did you want to smoke this thing?" Juice asked.

"Let's go inside." Mr. Slasher said.

The group followed Mr. Slasher inside, which seemed somehow much bigger than what they saw on the outside. John wondered if this was from all the years that he had people come out here and buy stuff from him or if he was already rich when he moved out here. There was quite a big living room with a stairway in the middle of the house leading up to the second floor. The living room had a fireplace with a large projector cover hanging just above it that looked twice as big as the current televisions sold at the store. It also seemed like there was a refrigerator in every single corner of the house on the first floor and each of them was massive in size.

"Wow, this place is huge." Juice said, looking up at what looked like the wooden version of a church ceiling.

"How does a place like this exist?" Janice asked.

"I started working on it about ten years ago when I came out here. I didn't like the idea that my log cabin made me feel like I was living back in the past, so I began expanding on it. Slowly I've made this place bigger." Mr. Slasher said.

John was beginning to like the man that they had come to see and he wasn't anything like what he previously thought the man to be. He had a rough welcome, but the man was generally nice to be around and having a massive indulgent-inducing house didn't hurt his personality either. The group sat down on the couch and Juice brought the joint to his lips.

"No, no. Let the newbie get the first burn." Mr. Slasher said.

"What?" Juice questioned but quickly complied with the man's steely gaze, "Alright, here Jonk."

Jonk grabbed the joint and looked at it, followed by looking at everyone else. She put it up to her lips and lit the joint, taking in a deep drag while the rest of them snickered. Jonk coughed and hacked as hard as she could as soon as the smoke hit the back of her throat.

"You never want to deep drag on the first go. You want to ease into it. Otherwise you'll get high too quickly and cough all the way there." Mr. Slasher said, as he grabbed the joint from her, "Anyway, how did you get the name of Jonk? That sounds like a rather weird nickname."

"Well, these guys gave it to me. John and Janice are the only ones without nicknames, and Juice came with his own nickname when he met John. It was when another arrogant nerd came up to me to argue about something. I don't remember what it was, I just know that it could not have been that important for me to have remembered it. Anyway, after I won the argument, John said that I was a nerd killer because I had completely destroyed him. At the time, he was obsessed with giving me a nickname because I was a tutor of his... still am actually. So, he started calling me the Judge of the Nerd Kings. When I told him to stop and that the nickname was way too long, he said Why not Jonk?, and I decided to let him have it."

"Wow, that's a weak story." Mr. Slasher said, passing the joint over to John.

"Well, you asked. So, you got the story." Jonk said.

"Well, if you live long enough I would suggest that you come up with something better."

"How did you get possessed?" Juice suddenly asked.

"What? Oh, well, my mother stabbed me." Mr. Slasher said, lifting up his shirt to show them his scar, "She stabbed me right here and as I was dying, I became possessed by Mr. Slasher."

"Wow, your mother stabbed you?" Janice asked, "What did you do?"

"What did I do?" Mr. Slasher asked, "You think I got stabbed because I was bad?"

"Well, I didn't mean to offend you but it sounds like you did something," Janice said.

"I'm going to kill you first." Mr. Slasher mumbled.

"What?" Janice asked, leaning in to hear him better.

"I said, sometimes you don't need to actually do anything to get stabbed. Sometimes people just don't want you to exist. Anyway, enough of this dark talk, I'm souring the mood. Let's talk about something else." Mr. Slasher said, quickly diverting the conversation.

The group continued to talk as the sun began to go down and night came about. Janice was the first one to nod off, then Jonk and John were next. The last one to fall asleep was Juice, who drifted off into a sound dream of food. Mr. Slasher got up from his seat and headed over to the kitchen, grabbing a knife. Then he came back over to the group, snickering as he heard the lot of them snoring. Quickly stabbing Janice in the trachea, he watched her eyes open in a panic as he held her down with a single hand. She gurgled as the blood quickly left her body and within moments she was peacefully asleep this time, but a much longer lasting sleep.

Mr. Slasher grabbed her hair and dragged her across the floor to the basement. He knew the kids would be out for quite a while, but he wanted to make sure to clean up the mess he made immediately so that he could be meticulous in his work. It didn't matter if the police looked for blood, this was, after all, listed as a hunting cabin but it would delay the amount of time the kids had to escape because they would only notice she was gone, not dead.

Mr. Slasher put her up on the table and went back upstairs with a mop bucket with some oxidized soap. Cleaning materials with oxidization took care of blood not only visibly but also, on an experiment he read the previous year, it made it harder for forensic investigators to find the traces. He looked at the others, seeing that they were all still sound asleep. He knew that kids were smart enough to travel in packs so it would have been weird for one of the friends to have gone off on their own. This meant he should go ahead and kill another one.

Mr. Slasher put his stuff against the couch and walked over to his hunting cabinet. He began to search through the drawers until he found his exotic animal hunting kit. Opening it, he pulled out one of the tranquilizers from the pack only to turn around and inject it inside of Juice. Juice woke up for a moment from the sudden pain of the needle and was confused, making a noise, but quickly fell back asleep. He put the dart back into the kit and closed the drawer. Then he took the time to clean up the bloody mess that he had made.

In the basement, Mr. Slasher put Juice on the table and closed the hidden steel door. The walls had been made sound proof so that no one could hear what went on inside. He strapped Juice down to the table, making sure the restraints were tight on his arms and head. He was still asleep and looked as peaceful as an angsting teenager could have been. This ended when Mr. Slasher drove an inch thick nail through Juice's arm and into the table. Juice immediately awoke, screaming in agony and trying hard to grab his arm but quickly finding that he was in restraints. Mr. Slasher walked over to the other side of the table and slammed another nail into the other arm. Juice screamed even louder this time. Juice would quickly bleed out from the wounds but he attempted to struggle as hard as he could to get free, getting blood everywhere. He attempted to talk to Mr. Slasher but the man didn't pay attention as he grabbed the buzzsaw that was attached to the ceiling. Juice screamed more and more, but that quickly came to a stop as Mr. Slasher pushed the saw through his throat and severed his head.

Mr. Slasher walked over to the table that had Janice on it and picked up the bone saw off of the side table. He began to cut the body into parts at the joints, ensuring that each limb that he cut off went into a zip lock bag, sucking out the air to delay decomposition. Placing most of the limbs inside of the refrigerator, he left out an arm, which he took his filet knife and began to slowly strip the meat off of the bone. After making sure all the meat had been stripped off, he put the bones inside of the vat of acid to let them dissolve. He washed off the meat, putting it inside of another zip lock bag. He would spend the rest of the night stripping the meat from the remainder of the body.

John awoke to the smell of meat cooking on the stove. Mr. Slasher was standing over the stove.

"That smells delicious." John said as he looked around, "Hey, where's Janice and Juice?"

"Oh, they said that they were going to go get food from the car." Mr. Slasher stated.

It was oddly cold inside of the house even though it was the middle of the summer. John got up and went to the window, looking outside to see that the sun was bright. For a moment, the sky flickered and John was taken aback. He looked closely, realizing that the window was looking into what seemed like a television screen. Then he began to hear the rain pelting the outside of the house.

"Do you have televisions projecting weather in the windows?" John asked.

"Yeah. I don't really like having to see the outside weather when it's raining really bad. Hey, if you wanna wake up your friend there I made some breakfast." Mr. Slasher said, turning to pour the meat onto a plate.

John looked over at Jonk, who was peacefully sleeping in a chair.

"Jonk!" John said loudly.

Jonk moaned and then turned over. John went over to her, shaking her on the shoulder.

"Jonk, wake up." John continued.

"What? Oh, hey John." Jonk said, stretching out her arms, "Where's Janice and Juice?"

"They went to the car." John said.

"Oh." Jonk said, her eyes filled with slight confusion.

"Mr. Slasher cooked us up something to eat." John said.

The three of them collected around the table, sitting down to enjoy the meal in front of them. John bit into the meat and was surprised at how good it tasted, with the fats mixing well with the meat. He had tasted something similar when he went overseas to one of the Japanese islands to train with his teacher.

"What type of meat is this Mr. Slasher?" John asked.

"It's imported. I got it in last night." Mr. Slasher said with a smile as he drank his cup of coffee.

The group ate in silence as the morning slowly passed them by. It was calmingly silent in the house, which was a much-appreciated joy John rarely had the opportunity to have. Jonk suddenly looked up from her plate at Mr. Slasher.

"So, what type of murderer was Mr. Slasher?" Jonk asked.

"Hmm?" Mr. Slasher questioned, looking at her with an eyebrow raised.

"I've been meaning to ask you ever since I heard it. You say that you are possessed by a man that was named Mr. Slasher and I was curious to know what type of murderer he was." Jonk asked, oddly excited in her question.

"Mr. Slasher was a cannibal, but he was known for slicing up his victims before he ate them. It took the police nearly five decades before they caught him and tried to charge him for his crimes. While he was in prison, some of the prison mates started to disappear around him and, when the police went to investigate, they found that he had hidden bones inside of the wall, but the meat was nowhere to be found. Even though they kept adding on years to his sentence, they eventually had to kill him in order to stop him from cannibalizing anyone else. It took three different cases of prison cannibalism in order for them to order an immediate death penalty. Within that time, he had killed and eaten at least twenty prison mates, and two guards." Mr. Slasher said with a smile, "Even though they killed him, they eventually had to shut down the prison he was in. Even though he was dead, prison mates claimed they were possessed by him and continued his lineage of cannibalism. By the time they closed down the prison and the cannibalism stopped, nearly half of all the prisoners had been eaten and the staff was reduced to a third of what it had been previously. We're actually eating breakfast over the land where the prison was."

John felt a slight chill run down his spine as he looked at Mr. Slasher and then slowly down at his plate. Up until that point, he had not really thought much about where their friends had gone, nor the size of the house, nor the crop of drugs, nor the amount of freezers that a strange man had stacked up. He had not thought about just how much of a trap the house really was and the story seemed to have activated some type of latent awareness in him.

"I think I'm going to go check on Janice and Juice, maybe help them carry the food up the path," John said, slowly getting up from the table and cleaning off his plate in the sink.

"Well, let me walk you out then." Mr. Slasher said, smiling as he got up from the table, leaving his unfinished plate on the table, "I need to go chop some wood anyway."

Mr. Slasher grabbed the ax off of the wall and followed John to the door. John went to go open the door but quickly found that it had been locked. He reached down to unlock the door but had a sudden pain in his head.

"Oh my gosh! John, no!" Jonk yelled, screaming in horror.

John felt dizzy for a moment and then quickly fell to the floor. Mr. Slasher pulled the ax out of his skull and dropped it to the side. Jonk tried to run to the back door but found that she couldn't open the door. Mr. Slasher carried John's dead body over to the basement door and opened the dumbwaiter. He shoved the body in the clean container he had already placed in there, lowering the dumbwaiter down into the basement. He picked up the mop bucket from the corner and began mopping up the blood. Meanwhile, Jonk was trying to smash through all of the windows but was quickly finding that each window had been covered with bullet proof walls of glass. She desperately ran up to the second level, hoping to find a place where she could get out of the building.

The doors were all blocked from the outside world by something on the other side and nothing would open. She went to the nearest place that had weapons inside of it, grabbing a gun and quickly loading it. Silence fell around her as Mr. Slasher had decided to let her be alone while he cleaned up the mess he had made. Jonk began to calm down from her frenzied panic. Just as she did, she noticed that the ceiling was cement, and not wooden, in the room that she was in. Remembering the story he had told them, she looked around at her surroundings. The bed was of a steel frame with a single mattress on it. There was a sink in the room along with a toilet. Mr. Slasher had not built on to a cabin, he had made a prison look like it was a log cabin.

The door opened and Jonk blasted all the bullets she had loaded into the weapon into the space the door opened up to. Mr. Slasher walked into the room as the gun made clicking noises. Jonk threw the gun at him but it didn't affect him. She got up to try and fight him, but the fist she threw at him was quickly caught. He twisted it and, like a twig, her wrist snapped. Just as she was about to scream, Mr. Slasher drove a long knife through her eyeball. Her body writhed for a moment as it quickly died and Mr. Slasher dragged her by the arm, out of the bedroom, and down into the basement.

Mr. Slasher's phone began to ring and he picked it up.

"Hello, Mr. Slasher here," he said. "Oh yeah, sure. I've got plenty... it's twenty dollars and just a good sit down is all I want... yeah. Five o'clock? Alright, I'll see you tomorrow. No problem. Alright, bye bye."

Mr. Slasher put Jonk's body on the table and close the door behind him.

COMPULSION

RONALD GOFF

Chapter One

Danny looked around the crime scene, looking for any sort of clue that he might have missed, anything that might stand out. But from everything he could see, this crime fit the pattern of the other sites he'd visited lately: there were no fingerprints or footprints left behind, no stray hairs or anything else that might contain DNA, and absolutely no way of tracing the murderer except the knowledge that he'd done this before and he'd do this again.

And the victims always fit the same pattern: young professionals from the medical field, and stunningly attractive ones at that.

"Danny, you ready to go?" his partner, Mark (but everyone called him by his last name, Lindsay), asked him.

Danny shook his head even though he knew he wasn't missing anything. "Lindsay, tell me her details again."

Lindsay sighed. "You already know them better than I do," he complained. But dutifully, he recited: "Name is Tracey Duncan. She was a nurse at the Park Hospital on South Street. Based on her time of death and the keys in the front door, we can assume that she had just got home from work when our killer attacked her. He grabbed her; she struggled—based on the bruises on her upper arms and the vase knocked over in the front hall. He subdued her and brought her up into her bedroom so he could tie her down on the bed. Then he strangled her." Lindsay paused. "The fact that all of his victims have been strangled is a bit odd still, don't you think? Shooting them all would be easier."

Danny shook his head. "There has to be a reason for it. Something deep and sick. Maybe he wants to be close enough to see the light go out in their eyes, or wants to feel them struggle against him, or wants to feel like he finally has power over them." He frowned and thought for a moment. "We need to figure out what all his victims have in common so we can stop him before the next one. There has to be some sort of a pattern."

"Well, Sherlock, you're not going to find anything else here," Lindsay said, a hint of impatience in his voice.

Danny frowned but finally shrugged and followed Lindsay wordlessly back to their car. Inside, he drummed his fingers restlessly against the dashboard. "I just can't shake the idea that there must be something that we're missing," he said. "In all the years that we've worked together, we've never let a guy get away with this many murders without catching him."

Lindsay shrugged. "This guy's smart, though—he clearly knows what he's doing."

"And the mark on their stomachs..." Danny said, pulling out a photo from his back pocket. The photo had been taken at the first of these crime scenes, but each new victim had the mark, always in the same place, just below their navel. One of the guys at the precinct had determined that the mark was being carved into their skin by the same knife each time, based on the similarities in the cuts. But there was no way of knowing if the cuts were made before or after the victim died.

"We've still had no luck in identifying it," Lindsay said grimly. "All we know is that it isn't a mark for any sort of mainstream religious or cult group." He glanced out the window. "Danny, we need to get back to the precinct—the rain is supposed to be strong tonight, and I don't want to be driving with buckets and buckets pouring down over my windshield."

"It's hurricane season," Danny said impatiently, still scanning the room for some other clue. "You've driven during hurricane season before." He walked over to the dresser and drummed his fingers on the top of it, then pulled open the top drawer. "People keep all sorts of things in their underwear drawers," he muttered, beginning to rifle through the woman's socks and panties.

"You have no respect for people's privacy," Lindsay muttered.

"She's dead anyway," Danny said dismissively. "I'm sure she doesn't mind me touching her…" He trailed off, pulling a photo out of the drawer. "Lindsay, look at this—what do you see?"

Lindsay came and squinted over his shoulder at the photo in Danny's hand. Then, he shrugged. "Typical breakup souvenir," he said. "A once-loving photo, with his face cut out of it."

"But look at his arms!" Danny insisted.

Lindsay frowned. "Well, yeah—typical once-loving photo: he's got his arms around her."

Danny made a disapproving noise. "Details, Lindsay. Look at the tattoos. If I'm not mistaken, they're the same type of rune as what's been carved into our victims stomachs—wouldn't you agree?"

Lindsay's eyebrows rose. "Are you telling me that she dated the creep who killed her? That would at least give him a motive. And that would mean the rune is likely some sort of signature. But what about all the other deaths? Surely he hasn't dated *all* of them."

Danny frowned. "We're going to need to dig back through some of these cases. And we're going to need to talk to Tracey's friends and see what we can find out about this guy."

Chapter Two

Unfortunately, finding out who the guy was proved to be more difficult than Danny expected it would be. First, there was the problem of tracking down anyone who knew Tracey outside of work. Because she was a young medical professional and kept long and irregular work hours, she seemed to mostly be friends with her coworkers—but none of them seemed to know even the most basic things about her personal life.

When they finally found Jenny Fisher, whom Tracey had known for her whole life and who frequently chatted with Tracey on the phone, Jenny didn't seem to know anything about the mystery boyfriend. She did concede that there probably had been a boyfriend based on Tracey's "desperate desire not to move cities after college", but she didn't know the guy's name.

Danny scowled down at the case file, wondering how anyone could live their life as such a mystery. *Why* was it that Jenny didn't know anything about Tracey's boyfriend? Had she been ashamed of him?

Could that be the reason he'd killed her?

Of course, even if they found the guy, there was no evidence linking him to the murders yet, but Danny couldn't seem to quit thinking that the guy in the photos must be the killer.

He rubbed at his eyes but jerked and looked guiltily at Lindsay when he knocked at the door. His partner folded his arms across his chest and frowned at him. "Danny, you should have gone home hours ago," he chided. "And you look like hell."

"You should have left home hours ago," Danny retorted. "And yet, you're still here as well."

"I'm *back* here," Lindsay said, falling into the seat across from Danny. "Allison called and said you were still here and that you looked like you might be preparing to sleep on the couch again."

Danny frowned. "It's none of Allison's business if I want to sleep on my couch."

"It is if you overwork yourself into an early grave," Lindsay said. "You're one of the best detectives on the team; they need you around here. And if you keep obsessing about the case like this, you know the Commander is going to take you off it."

Danny's lips tightened into a thin line. "He wouldn't do that. Not when I'm this close to figuring it out. If I could just figure out..." Suddenly, he turned to his computer and started typing rapidly. "The tattoos. He couldn't have done those on his own—not with the way they spiral around his arms. If we could just find someone who did the tattoos, they would have to have a record of him, they might even have contact info for him." He chewed at the edge of his fingernail as he waited for the results to load.

Lindsay snorted. "What are you searching, 'rune tattoos Miami'? The guy could have gotten those tattoos done anywhere, you know."

"Tracey didn't have time to travel, and her friend Jenny said she was desperate to stay here in Miami after she finished college and that it was probably to do with a boyfriend. We can assume that means the boyfriend is from Miami and that they never travelled together," Danny said absently. He grinned at the screen. "And sure enough..."

He quickly printed the shop's sample pictures as well as their main page. "I have a field trip to take," he said.

Lindsay snorted, clicking through the screen as well. "Tomorrow, maybe," he said. "They're only open until 8:00—it's nearly 9:30 now."

Danny scowled at the webpage and then sank down into his seat. "I guess it's time to call it a night," he said, sighing.

"I guess it's time," Lindsay agreed, smiling fondly at the man. "Let's get you home, all right? Again, it doesn't benefit any of us if you burn yourself out."

Chapter Three

The next day, they were both there just before when the shop opened at noon. Lindsay snorted at Danny's jeans and faded black teeshirt. "You don't look even remotely like the type of person who would get a tattoo, even dressed like that," he pointed out. "You're definitely not going to be able to convince the guy that you want some strange runes tattooed up your arm, especially since you don't even know what they mean."

"Well, what do you suggest?" Danny snapped irritably. "It's not like *you* look like the type of person to get a tattoo; you're too blonde and clean-cut and all-American."

"Here, let me see," Lindsay said, leaning over to pull open the dashboard. He rummaged around for a minute and then came out with an eyeliner pencil. "Jane's got half her makeup kit here in my glove compartment," he said ruefully. "Now look at me and close your eyes."

"You're *not* putting eyeliner on me," Danny protested.

"What if that's the only way to get the information that you need?" Lindsay asked.

Danny frowned and then snagged the eyeliner pencil from Lindsay's hand. "Fine," he muttered. "But I'm going to do it myself. I don't trust your big oaf hands not to stab me in the eye with this thing, and that's going to be a big setback to my case."

Lindsay snorted and watched with amusement as Danny began to outline his eyes with careful strokes. "You'll need it a bit thicker than that to look like a good emo kid," he critiqued.

Danny scowled but dutifully smeared on more of the black and smudged it around with his fingertips. "Better?" he asked.

Lindsay grinned. "Looks lovely. Makes your eyes pop." He reached over and messed up Danny's hair a little more. "Perfect. Now throw that back in the dashboard and let's get this over with."

Danny sighed and hopped out of the car, heading quickly into the shop. There was a woman with full sleeve tattoos and bubblegum-pink hair leaning against the counter reading a magazine. She eyed the two of them critically. "I have an appointment at 12:15," she told them. "Granted he's usually a bit late, but I don't have time to tattoo either of you now." She snapped her gum and turned back to the magazine.

Danny moved hesitantly forward. "Do you have time to do a bit of a...consultation, maybe? I'm not quite sure what I want yet, but I was hoping maybe I could talk to you and get a better idea before I start drawing it all out."

The woman—Amelia, according to her name tag—frowned at him. "You're going to draw your own tattoo?" she asked skeptically. "For your first tattoo?"

"I'm an art student," Danny lied. "And I want something that's going to be unique and personal to me. Something that'll tell my story."

Amelia rolled her eyes. "Of course you do. Do you realize how many years a good tattoo artist has to practice to be a good tattoo artist? Drawing designs is one thing, but having an understanding of anatomy and being able to fit pieces on a body is another thing entirely."

"I know," Danny said. "That's part of why I just wanted to talk it over with you, if you have a moment."

Amelia sighed. "Fine. Fifteen minutes. Do you have *any* idea what you want?"

Danny pulled out the crumpled print-out and smoothed it out over the counter. "I saw this on your website, and that's part of why I came here. I like the idea of doing something with runes—something that maybe I understand that no one else understands. Or very few people anyway. I like the idea of expressing myself like that, but kind of in secret."

Lindsay stared at Danny with new appreciation: he knew the man had done a lot of undercover work in the past, but he had never realized the man was this good at thinking on his feet.

"I remember this guy," Amelia said, nodding at the picture. "I can't remember what he said the runes meant, but same as you, he wanted to design his own tattoo. He actually did a pretty good job of it—but it's all runes, no pictures, and that makes things a little easier. We adjusted a couple of them so they lay better around the curvature of his arm, but for the most part, he had a good understanding of how things were going to work."

"Do you know what type of runes these are?" Lindsay asked curiously. "Did he make them up himself?"

Amelia glanced over at him and shrugged. "Honestly, no idea. Most of the people who come here want to personalize their tattoos—we don't draw the butterflies and dreamcatchers clientele. But because of that, a lot of the tattoos have private meaning, and it's not really our place to ask for their life story while they're being tattooed."

Danny traced one of the runes with his finger. "Do you have any contact information for him?" he asked. "I know that would maybe be kind of a breach of security for you to give me his information, but maybe I could have you pass my information on to him? I'd love to talk to him about designing my tattoo if he had a moment."

Amelia frowned and drummed her fingers on the countertop. "I'm sure we have contact info for him, but we keep a specific list of people who agree to be contacted in the future if people have questions about their tattoos. I'll have to check if he's on it. And even if it is, we may not have current contact details for him—you know how people change phone numbers and email addresses these days..."

"Oh man, if you have his info, that'd be great," Danny enthused. "Like I said, when I saw those pictures on your website, well—that's what really brought me here."

The phone rang, and Amelia reached over the counter to answer it. She looked momentarily startled, and Danny listened with half an ear to her conversation while he tried to think through anything else about this case that he might be missing.

He tuned back in quickly, though, as Amelie said, "Well, you wouldn't believe it, but I've actually got two guys here in the shop at the moment who were interested in the last work we did for you, the sleeve of runes, and they were wondering if they could talk to you about that. Maybe we could schedule a time that would work for all of us?"

Surely it was too much of a coincidence for him to call at the same time as they were there in the shop. Danny whipped his head towards the door, wondering if they were being followed—but surely one of them would have noticed that, if that were the case. There were plenty of places the guy could be hiding, though: in the cars in the parking lot, in the strip mall across the street, or in half a dozen places in between.

His gut instinct was that they needed to get out of there, but he wasn't willing to leave without the information. They were close enough now that he could practically taste it, and after months of chasing this guy, he couldn't leave. But... He glanced sidelong at Lindsay, trying to remind himself that it wasn't just his own life he would be putting in danger by staying. But then again, Lindsay knew the risks just as well as he did.

"How about today at 3:30?" Amelia asked, looking at Danny for confirmation. "You could come into the shop and do your consultation, and then around 4:00, you could meet up with these guys and chat." She paused, listening. "Okay. Okay, sure. Sounds great."

She hung up at the phone and clapped her hands together. "Well, that was a bit of weirdness from the universe: that was the guy with the rune tattoos on the phone, as I'm sure you could hear. He's looking to come in for a consultation as he designs his latest tattoo—a piece to commemorate a special someone that he's just lost." She made shooing motions with her hands. "So come back here around 4:00 today and you can have your talk. But now, my 12:15 appointment is here."

"Thanks," Danny said, grabbing the print-out and heading towards the door with Lindsay on his heels. In the car, he heaved a sigh. "We're going to need backup, I think."

Chapter Four

"There's no way I'm letting the two of you continue to work this case if you think your lives are in danger," the Commander snapped when Danny requested backup for that afternoon. "Do you realize what a shitshow of paperwork we would have on our hands if the two of you were shot while investigating this guy—especially if anyone found out you *knew* you were being followed? And the last thing I need is for the two of you, some of our best detectives, to get killed in the line of duty."

"You can't take us off the case," Danny complained, rubbing at his eyes, heedless of the way it smeared around the eyeliner that he still had yet to remove. "We're *this* close to getting it solved, and if we can meet up with this guy tonight, then–"

"We don't even know if he's the guy we want, Danny," Lindsay reminded him gently. "Sure, there's a striking resemblance between the runes on his arms and the runes that have been carved into the women's stomachs, but that doesn't actually amount to solid evidence. For all we know, this is still tied to some sort of cult or religion that, however minor, might have more than one follower who uses these runes."

Danny dropped into a chair, hands over his face. "I can't let this one go, though," he mumbled.

The Commander frowned. "All the more reason for me to remove the two of you from this case," he said. "Stupid mistakes get made when you get obsessive."

"There's nothing you can do to stop me from going to that tattoo parlor tonight," Danny told him. "Take me off the case—fire me, if you want to. But I'm going there, and I'm going to talk to the guy. There's nothing you can do to stop me."

For a long moment, Danny and the Commander stared at one another. "I'm going as well," Lindsay said, breaking the silence. Both the others swiveled to face him, and he shrugged. "I know Danny well enough to know that he's going to go. And he's going to need backup. It would look weird for him to have shown up with me earlier in the morning and then show up with someone else in the afternoon. So I'm going with him. And there's nothing you can do to stop me either." He paused and gave them a weird smile. "You know, my kid sister is a young, female, medical professional. Doesn't live in Miami, but I can't help thinking..."

The Commander threw his hands in the air. "I knew the two of you were going to crack eventually," he said. "Well, it's your funeral. But if you get killed..."

"Not in my plan for the night," Danny said tersely. "But you'll arrange for us to have backup?"

"Of course," the Commander said, sighing.

When they entered the tattoo parlor that afternoon, Danny felt like he was practically buzzing with adrenaline. Between knowing the danger they could be in and knowing that they were this close to solving the case... For a moment, as he stared wordlessly at the man in the back of the shop, his tattooed arms moving animatedly as he talked with Amelia.

Then, he shook his head and moved forward, a grin on his face. "Hey, those tattoos look even cooler in person than they did on the online pictures," he said cheerfully. He stuck out his hand. "Good to meet you. I'm Danny."

The guy reached out his hand and shook Danny's giving him a curious once-over. "Chris," he said. "Look, not to be a dick, but you don't really look like the kind of guy that would get a bunch of tattoos up his arm."

Danny ducked his head. "I'm going through a bit of a transitional period at the moment," he said. "I blame it on my mother; she was Southern, so she raised me to be a good guy in sweaters and slacks. I'm still discovering who I really am."

Lindsay fought not to snort at the story—he knew Danny's mother, and she was definitely not a church-going Southern woman. Fortunately, he managed to suppress the noise.

And the story had Chris nodding. "I feel that, man. Maybe you can work that into the tattoo somehow. Amelia said you had some questions about it, though?"

"Yeah." Danny glanced over at Amelia. "Look, I'm sure you have other appointments coming in, right? Maybe we should get out of your hair. There's a coffeeshop around the corner where we could talk." If things got messy, he didn't want her to be in the thick of it.

Amelia shrugged. "Up to you what you want to do. But yeah, I do have another guy coming in soon. And if you want more input from me, sorry, but you'll have to pay a consultation fee just like anyone else."

Danny grinned. "No problem; I totally get that." He held out a hand to her. "Look, it was great meeting you, and thanks for putting us in contact with one another. I'm sure you'll see me back."

At the coffeeshop, they each ordered drinks and tossed their jackets across the backs of their chairs. "So what were your questions, then?" Chris asked Danny.

Danny frowned and flipped his badge out. "I have a couple questions for you regarding the death of Ms. Tracey Duncan. Don't make me take you down to the station first. We do have backup surrounding us."

Chris' eyes widened a bit, but he didn't protest. "What do you want to know?"

"Let's start with something simple," Lindsay suggested. "How did you know Tracey?"

"We met in an art class back during her sophomore year," Chris said. "Tracey's parents always wanted her to be a doctor, but she wasn't so sure about it. So she decided to experiment and take a couple fun classes in her free time." He gave a soft smile. "She loved that art class." There was a clap of thunder, and he glanced skywards for a moment before continuing. "Anyway, we hit it off really well and started dating not too long after that."

"When did she break up with you?" Danny asked.

Chris raised his eyebrows. "She never broke up with me," he said. "We were going to get married next fall."

"She didn't wear a wedding band."

"No," Chris agreed, looking embarrassed. "When I proposed to her, I couldn't afford a good engagement ring, so I proposed with a locket that had our faces both in it. I thought it was sweet. I'm an artist, so I don't make a lot. And because she's new in the medical realm, she doesn't make that much either, and she has a lot of student loans to pay off. Eventually, we decided that rather than put money into an engagement band that she won't wear after the wedding anyway, we might as well put that money into the honeymoon and do something really special. So there was never an engagement band."

"She wasn't wearing a locket either," Danny said.

Chris reached into his pocket and pulled out a small necklace on a silver chain. "She left this at my place the last time she was there—not because she was breaking up with me or anything like that; she just forgot it. The locket itself is solid sterling silver, but the chain isn't, so it started to fade to copper when she wore it in the shower. She usually took it off to shower and then put it back on immediately afterwards, but that day, the hospital called her in early, and in her rush to get there, she forgot to put it back on."

"Hmm," Danny said.

"You don't seem too heartbroken for someone who just lost his fiancée," Lindsay remarked.

Chris looked at him for a long moment. "Well, what am I supposed to do?" he asked. "You trick me here under the impression that you want to talk about tattoos, and instead you want to ask me questions about this crappy act of the universe." He frowned at them. "I hope you don't think I killed her or something—that would be sick."

Danny raised an eyebrow at him and wordlessly pulled the picture out of his pocket. "Judging by the way your face is cut out of this picture, we assumed the two of you had broken up. But perhaps it's just that she didn't feel the same way about you but didn't have the guts to end things? Maybe once you found out, that made you–"

"Stop," Chris said, pressing his fingertips against his eyelids. "Jesus, just *stop*. I didn't kill her, okay? You want to know why my face was cut out of that picture? That's the one I used for the locket. Look, you can still see her hair brushing my shoulder in the picture here." He popped open the locket, and sure enough, it was clear from the hair and from the scissor marks at the edge of the picture that it was the same picture. "I don't know where you got that from, but I'm telling you, I didn't kill her."

"But the runes on your arms," Danny protested weakly. "And the fact that you called the tattoo parlor at the same time that we were there..."

"I didn't kill her," Chris repeated. He scowled. "But if you have a minute, I might be able to give you a lead on who did."

Chapter Five

"Wish we could have searched his bag," Danny muttered under his breath as he and Lindsay drove back towards the precinct.

Lindsay gaped over at him. "You still think he was the murderer," he said incredulously. "After all that–"

"We need to look up links between this guy and the other women," Danny interrupted. "I know you want to get home to your wife, but do you think it could wait for a couple hours? There has to be something there that we're missing. It's not enough that they're all young, female medical practitioners. There has to be something more to it. And the runes..."

"Chris says he made up those runes," Lindsay reminded him.

"He can't have," Danny muttered. "Or else our killer didn't make up the runes and copied them from..." He trailed off, the idea suddenly striking him. "Or else our killer copied him."

"So great, our killer is anyone who has ever seen the tattoo parlor's website," Lindsay said sarcastically. "Give it a rest, Danny. We need to start focusing on other cases. As the Commander said, your fixation with this is unhealthy, and that can lead to mistakes. You were ready to convict an innocent man in there today."

Danny drummed his fingers on the steering wheel, peering out through the pounding rain. "Gut feeling is still telling me that we're so close to solving it, though," he said. "We *have* to be." He glanced over at his partner. "Based on what you said about your kid sister, why aren't you more obsessed with this case?"

"Based on the fact that you don't have a kid sister, why are you so obsessed with this case?" Lindsay retorted. "And keep your eyes on the road. You know how I feel about driving during rains like these."

Danny smiled a little, but his face quickly turned thoughtful again. "Who would have seen Chris' tattoos and also known his girlfriend?" he asked. "Anyone in their friend circle. But why target medical professionals? It had to have been someone who–"

"Had an unhealthy fixation on Tracey," Lindsay suggested. "Anyone who was fixated on Chris would have gone after him. But someone who was fixated on Tracey would have gone after other people in the hopes that they could get to her enough that she'd break up with Chris and be with him."

"What's the significance of the number twelve?" Danny asked. "That's how many women we've had who fit the match at this point."

"Twelve months in a year?" Lindsay suggested. "A year ago... Hurricane season. We would have had Hurricane Jerica. We need to know where Tracey was then." He frowned. "But if Tracey's dead now, it could be that the killer won't kill anyone else, right?"

"Doesn't matter," Danny said grimly. "He still deserves to stand for his actions." He paused. "There was a journal at the crime scene. In her underwear drawer." He pulled the small black notebook out of his pocket and tossed it to Lindsay. "It doesn't say anything incriminating, otherwise I would have mentioned it before. But what was our girl doing twelve months ago from the night she was killed?"

Lindsay stared at his partner for a long moment but then flipped open the journal, reminding himself of what Danny had said the night of the murder: the woman was already dead. Her privacy hardly mattered anymore, and anyway, they were trying to allow her to rest in peace or save future women or whatever. He took a deep breath and began to read, aided by the light of his phone.

When he found the correct date, his eyes practically bugged out of his head. "Pull over," he said. "You're going to want to see this."

"I can't pull over on the side of the highway during hurricane season," Danny said impatiently. He did pull off the next exit, though, and stopped in a gas station parking lot, flicking on the overhead lights. "Now give me that thing." He flipped to the right page and began reading. "Shit."

Went home with Skipper tonight. Thing is, I know Chris loves me and wants to marry me, but I've still always had this lingering doubt, and Skipper plays right into that. It's not just in bed, although that's a large part of it. We just seem to click, in a way that Chris and I have never managed. And where Chris makes me feel like I need to be a better person, Skip makes me feel like I can be the best version of myself and he'll always love me. I'm going to have to figure out what to do long-term, but tonight, I was promising Skip that I'd break it off with Chris and be his forever...

Danny frantically skipped forwards and backwards in the journal, but that was the only mention of 'Skipper' that he could find. He pulled out a phone and quickly dialed a number that he had memorized.

"Who are you calling?" Lindsay asked.

Danny held up one finger, telling him to wait. "Jenny? This is Detective Carlson." he asked when the woman answered. "What can you tell me about a guy named Skipper?"

There was a sharp intake of breath on the other end of the line. "What do you know about Skipper?" she asked.

Danny raised an eyebrow. "Not much," he admitted. "Except that I know that he knows Tracey. And I'm not sure how."

"We went to school with him," Jenny said faintly. "Tracey dated him for a little while, before she went off to college. But it was nothing serious—at least for Tracey, it wasn't." She paused with a frown. "You don't think Skip had anything to do with Tracey's death, do you?"

"What was their relationship like?" Danny asked, ignoring her question.

Jenny paused. "Well, like I said, the relationship was probably more serious to Skip than it was to Tracey, but still, he couldn't have had anything to do with Tracey's death—he loved her. He wanted to win her back, I'm sure, but he wouldn't have killed her, unless he thought there was absolutely no way he could ever have her again."

Danny listened to her words with a sinking heart. "Jenny, do you have any sort of contact for Skipper? Or even a last name? I have some questions for him."

He could tell Jenny was crying when she responded. "He wouldn't have done that," she insisted. "I swear it. But if you need to talk to him, his phone number is 234-871-1919." She hung up before he could ask any further questions.

Danny himself hung up the phone with shaking fingers and looked over at Lindsay in the passenger's seat. "I think we've just solved the case," he said, but he didn't feel as exhilarated as he'd expected.

Epilogue

Sure enough, the more they looked into Skipper Willkinson's history, the more likely it seemed that he was Tracey's murderer. And the more likely it seemed that the other women had not been random targets. It went beyond being young, female, and a medical professional—Skip had known them all. One of them, he'd met at a bar. Another, he'd dated briefly. A third had been Tracey's roommate the year that Skipper had visited Tracey at university. And so on.

Danny heard the sentencing read out in the courtroom, feeling utterly numb. He was glad they'd finally gotten justice, of course, but he still didn't feel good about the whole thing, especially not when he saw Jenny crying over to one side. He looked over at Lindsay and gave him a silent signal to show he was leaving the room the back way. There would be too many reporters in the front, and although he normally would have answered their questions, today he didn't have the heart.

Lindsay followed him.

"You okay, Danny?" the man asked.

Danny shrugged and then shook his head. "I don't know that I can do this anymore," he admitted. "It's not just obsessing about cases. I could work through that. But it's..."

Lindsay laid a hand on his shoulder as he trailed off, squeezing lightly. "You don't have to tell me," he said. "I know. I can see it in you. I've known it for longer than you have, I think." He paused. "What are you going to do instead?"

Danny smiled bitterly. "Not sure," he admitted. "I worked my whole life for this. Which is part of why I can't do this anymore, I guess. Skipper worked his whole life to be with Tracey, didn't he? And look where that got him in the end. Maybe any amount of fixation is a bad thing."

Lindsay snorted. "I don't think picking the perfect occupation for yourself is necessarily going to make you a serial killer," he said.

"We never did figure out what those runes meant," Danny said. "I always wanted to ask, but instead, we were too busy asking about the deaths."

"It was the same mark as on the front of Tracey's locker," Lindsay said. "I'm surprised you didn't realize. I asked Chris about it at one point and he just smirked and said he had dropped a bunch of spaghetti noodles on the floor the night of their first real date and that was the pattern they all fell into."

Danny took a shaky breath. "You better train your next partner well," he said finally, staring out at the street rather than looking at Lindsay. "And don't get yourself killed."

"Should be easier now my partner isn't crazy," Lindsay teased, clapping a hand on Danny's shoulder. "I'll see you when you're stir-crazy and ready to come back."